Neil Armstrong in North Somerset

and more than 50 other short tales for a fast world

Jack Lethbridge

Copyright © 2017 Jack Lethbridge

The moral right of the author has been asserted.

Apart from any fair dealing for the purposes of research or private study, or criticism or review, as permitted under the Copyright, Designs and Patents Act 1988, this publication may only be reproduced, stored or transmitted, in any form or by any means, with the prior permission in writing of the publishers, or in the case of reprographic reproduction in accordance with the terms of licences issued by the Copyright Licensing Agency. Enquiries concerning reproduction outside those terms should be sent to the publishers.

Matador
9 Priory Business Park,
Wistow Road, Kibworth Beauchamp,
Leicestershire. LE8 0RX
Tel: (+44) 116 279 2299
Fax: (+44) 116 279 2277
Email: books@troubador.co.uk
Web: www.troubador.co.uk/matador

ISBN 9781788039468

Cover design 'Head' by Amanda Bond inspired by Cleo Mussi

British Library Cataloguing in Publication Data.
A catalogue record for this book is available from the British Library.

Printed and bound in Great Britain by 4edge Limited
Typeset in 10.5pt Minion Pro by Troubador Publishing Ltd, Leicester, UK

Matador is an imprint of Troubador Publishing Ltd

Neil Armstrong in North Somerset

For Amanda
for Head/Space

Contents

Foreword: Lives on the Winds   xi

PART 1 – FLASHES   1
1. Neil Armstrong in North Somerset   3
2. Rules of the Lido   7
3. The Man in This Story   11
4. Passing over Paradise   13
5. Lament for the Yellow Labelled Professor   15
6. On the Perilous Edge   17
7. Whose Tomorrow?   19
8. The Miracle of the Ladder   21
9. True Blue   23
10. Still   25
11. Schrödinger's Other Cat   27
12. Dips   29
13. The Second One   31
14. The Price of a Normal Life   33
15. Aftermath   35
16. The Chosen One   37
17. A Bigger, Heavier Thing   39
18. Red Fluff   41
19. Enduring, with Gentle Bitterness   43
20. Enough to Wake the Dead   47
21. Once   49

22.	Charming and Naïve	51
23.	The Day That Happened	53
24.	A Lifetime	55
25.	Justin Kershaw: A Life in Books	57
26.	Paris No Sale	59
27.	After the Fall	61
28.	Fortune	65
29.	The Name	67
30.	Eye for I	71
31.	Janey's Book of Many Faces	73
32.	How I Acquired a Decent Suit	75
33.	Post, Nail, Thieves…?	77
34.	At the End of the Day	79
35.	Making do	81
36.	The Third Man on the Moon	83
37.	I'm Glad a Crusty Stole Your Pizza	85
38.	Sky Blue	87
39.	Our Little Jaunt	89
40.	I am not a Goldfish	93
41.	On Beauty	95
42.	Taken to the Brink – a Book Idea	97
43.	Is There Anybody Not Waiting?	101
44.	The Sensible Ending	103
	PART 2 – SHORTS	105
45.	The Taxi Driver's Husband	107
46.	The Boy Who Was Born Without a Heart	119
47.	Serious 'Cider	127
48.	Jernees End	137
49.	Lobster Tails	145
50.	Say Hello to Ravi	151

51.	The Leafcutter Ant	165
52.	A Point in the Middle	177
53.	The Drive	191
54.	Voices on the Beach	199
55.	Life in the Chalet	211

Foreword

Lives on the Winds

If ever you find yourself standing in an open space on a windy day, turn your face to the wind and listen, very carefully. Hear anything? Probably not.

So close your eyes and listen again. Chances are, if you're anything like me, you will hear voices. Not at first maybe, there will just be faint sounds, hard to discern from the droning of the wind itself. Indeterminate sounds, at first, but then gradually, if you are patient, as your ears tune into these sounds, they will coalesce as voices. You have to listen carefully, but they are there, I promise. Voices of people, like you and me, living out their lives on the winds.

They are not here of course, these people, these lives, they are not here in this open space with you, they are somewhere else, far away possibly, but you are here, this is where you are listening from, this open space. So don't be fooled, they are your voices, your people, living out their lives for you, here and now, on the winds where you're standing. They may be far away but their voices are here and they stay with us for a time, until they pass on somewhere else, to find other listeners maybe, who knows? The voices come and go, as the winds rise and fall, and when they return it's often different voices, a different conversation, a new story, or at least a glimpse of a story. But that's OK, isn't it?

If you're not sure about all this, let me share my voices with you, these lives on the winds that I listen to while I wait. Keep me company for a while, and we can listen together, while it's still light and the wind is not yet too cold. Stay with me if you can, it won't be for long, and I need to share these voices. I don't always understand what they are saying, even when I can hear the words, and having someone else to listen with me would help, I'm sure. Sometimes their stories make sense and sometimes they don't. But maybe they will to you, or maybe between us we can make sense of them. That would be good.

We can stand here together dipping in and out of people's lives. Or maybe it's them dipping in and out of ours?

Part 1

Flashes

Neil Armstrong in North Somerset

It's an unlikely story I'll admit, the first man to walk on the moon turning up at our village pub in North Somerset almost unrecognised twenty years on (this was 1989). He may have been there for quite a while before anyone noticed, but I guess the price of being the first human to set foot on another world is that someone is bound to recognise you sooner or later, wherever you go. I'm just surprised it was Jim who spotted him.

'Ere Joe, ain't that the bloke what went to the moon? You know the feller. One small step and all that. Whatsisname?'

'Neil Armstrong?'

'That's the feller, Armstrong.'

'Where?'

'Over there, by the clock. Tall chap. Bald head.'

'Looks a bit like him.'

'It is him, I tell you. Just been in the bog with him. Recognise those feet anywhere.'

'What's he doing here then Jim?'

'That's what I'd like to know.'

Others seemed less sure.

'Neil who?'

'Armstrong. Neil Armstrong. First man on the moon. One small step and all that.'

'How do you know that's him, Jim?'
'Cause I do. I've seen his picture.'
'What, without his helmet on?'
'Of course.'
'I thought he had to keep his helmet on.'
'Yeh, on the moon, of course, but not down here, yer daft bleeder.'

Naturally, there was an explanation. A guy who lived in one of the grander houses worked for the European Space Agency and had arranged a visit by the astronaut as part of a PR exercise. Unsure how to entertain the great man, his host thought a drop of cider in a quaint village pub might be of interest, which indeed it was. Apparently he consumed several pints of our local brew, a cloudy, greenish liquid guaranteed to give the unsuspecting drinker a restless and sweaty night. I doubt even Neil Armstrong had endured greater discomforts.

So why has this story never been told before? Those feet, here in England's green and pleasant land? Maybe the sparse coverage in the press. A short item did feature in the *North Somerset Gazette*, but went largely unnoticed. This may have been because it appeared near the bottom of the inside back page, buried in the sports section, with the ambiguous title:

Moon man barred as Priory enjoy darts victory

On Friday, regulars of the Half Moon in Shapwick were surprised to find astronaut Neil Armstrong among their number. After an enjoyable evening sampling the local brew, Neil, 52 from Carolina, USA, was invited to take part in a darts match against local rivals, the Priory in Glastonbury. However, following an appeal by the Priory, Mr Armstrong was deemed ineligible under the residency rules of the North Somerset Darts League. The Priory won a closely fought contest 6 – 5.

It may not seem much compared to the front page of *Time* magazine, but it is still there for all to see on the *Gazette* website (www.northsomersetgazette.co.uk/archive/1989).

There forever, like that first footprint on the moon.

Rules of the Lido

1. This is not a lido.

    It was, once, but is now a private health spa in all but retro-name. The pool's still there, exposed to the elements, but solar heated these days to take the chill off.

2. Introduce a new member and receive 10% off your membership.

    Gayle, my fellow Stitch and Bitcher, introduced me. 'You'll love it, dear, you'll feel a new woman.' Thank you Gayle, how right you were.

3. No diving.

    Especially in at the deep end. Will I never learn?

4. Please take a shower before entering the pool.

    A cold one, I would suggest.

5. Adults only in the jacuzzi.

It should say, 'please behave like an adult in the jacuzzi, not like a teenager'. Take note, lady, though you're not entirely to blame, it takes two to entangle. And it's not easy to ignore the effects of a powerful jet of water probing your nether regions while you gaze up into the naked night sky. As you were quick to point out, as you touched my leg.

6. No heavy petting.

   It doesn't say that of course, far too classy, but it should. Though I've never been sure what it means – when does light petting turn into heavy? But lines are drawn, and easily transgressed it seems. Did I pet you, or you me? Was I your pet, or you mine?

7. Please remove your clothes from the changing cubicle so that others can use it.

   That's remove *your* clothes *from* the changing cubicle, lady, not *my* clothes *in* the changing cubicle (well my costume anyway). But I accept the hot shower was enticing after we'd cooled off in the pool. It was hard not to feel alive for once, and I am easily led, ask anyone. You said my skin was 'raw as silk' and I can never resist a poet.

8. Please leave your valuables in the lockable cupboards next to Reception.

   Why? Just when I needed my guard, you know the one

that protects me from the likes of you, but most of all from myself. I carry it with me everywhere, normally. Never leave your valuables too far away, I say.

9. Renew your membership immediately and receive a 10% discount.

    Tempting, but no thanks. I don't object to the lido, it's just not my sort of place. Even with solar heating the pool is still cold. An open air jacuzzi is all well and good but not when it rains. And the cubicles are nicely private but rather cramped. As for the clientele, well they're not a bad lot, but maybe not really my type. Why? Well, let's just say I don't trust people who leave their valuables in locked cupboards – apart from anything else they clearly don't trust me. Gayle should have warned me. There's stitching and bitching for you.

10. There are no rules.

    You have to make them up for yourself.

The Man in This Story

(L'homme dans cette histoire)

Once, I met a writer in a bar who told me she was writing a story and would like to include our conversation.

'What conversation?' I asked.

'The one we're having now,' she said.

'Oh I see. Yes, of course.'

Suddenly, I felt self-conscious and our conversation dried up. I apologised.

'That's OK,' she said, 'the conversation we've already had will do. It's only a short story.'

Later, she sent me a copy of her story and I thought, 'how strange, I don't recognise this person in the story, even though he has my name'.

So I told the writer who said to me, 'Don't worry, he's not really you. You are you, this is someone else I created for this story.'

She smiled politely but nervously, like I was some stranger she had once met in a bar who then turned up out of the blue one day to continue the conversation.

'OK,' I said, although when I read it again, this person did seem strangely familiar. After all, he spoke words I had spoken, in a conversation I remember having, with a writer I once met in a bar.

And so I began to wonder whether he was me after all, that maybe I really was the man in the story. It made sense. It still does. Maybe I am him all the time, here in this story for anyone to read, at any time and maybe forever. How scary is that?

(Translated from the French)

Passing over Paradise

Fuelled by regret, Adam boarded the 6am flight from Sydney heading for London. At the same moment, though not the same time, Eve took off from Heathrow on her way to Sydney. It had been a difficult separation; they both felt moved to make a grand gesture.

Somewhere over Iraq the two planes crossed. Eve wondered if she was wise to try and rekindle a relationship with a man who'd chosen to accept a job 10,000 miles away. 'Maybe he'll freak out, think I'm desperate,' she thought, biting an apple.

At the same moment, at the same time, on Adam's plane his neighbour said, 'The Garden of Eden is down there somewhere, between the Euphrates and the Tigris. That's where they think it was.' Adam looked out the window hoping for a glimpse of Paradise. There was nothing to see but grey cloud.

On arrival at Heathrow, Adam headed for Eve's house and found it empty. Her mother, who lived nearby, said 'Eve's gone to Sydney. She thought she would surprise you.' 'She has,' he said. 'Why don't you come in?' said Eve's mother and smiled kindly. She'd always liked Adam.

Eve, confronted by Adam's housemate Tom, despaired. 'How could he be so stupid?' she said. 'I think he meant well,' said Tom, 'you can have his room until he gets back if you like.' 'Or share mine,' he added mischievously. 'I think I'll find a hotel,' said Eve, but didn't.

On their return journeys they agreed to fly at the same time, to avoid embarrassment. Eve was excited by the prospect of showing Tom her family home, the orchards of her childhood she had enthused about. Over Iraq, Adam said to Eve's mother, 'The Garden of Eden is down there somewhere, but don't bother looking for it.'

Lament for the Yellow Labelled Professor

It was innocent enough, the Saturday night dash to Tesco's to grab yellow labelled bargains. I did wonder if the petrol costs outweighed the savings, but you did the calculations (you're not a mathematician for nothing) and reckoned it was worth it.

I saw the pleasure you took from hunting down those dented tins and barely bruised fruit. '"Best before" is not the same as "use by"!' We weren't well off, the children were small and I couldn't work much. I enjoyed the challenge of conjuring dinner from unpredictable ingredients. It usually worked out OK.

But then, the doubts. This had lasted for years, and we weren't badly off anymore. You'd been promoted, I was working more and fancied a Saturday night out occasionally. But nothing could thwart your run to the supermarket before closing time. More ritual than habit.

I wouldn't have minded if the benefits were evident. A new bed, perhaps, which we needed, desperately. 'No point making all this effort to save money if you're going to fritter it away.'

Finally, it got too much. The bananas on Christmas Eve did it. I was used to the annual turkey run, the last-minute trip for a left-over bird at a knock down price. But when you came home, boot full of overripe bananas, I despaired. 'Your mum loves bananas. Only a pound, the lot!'

I still have that photo of my mum surrounded by bunches of bananas, smiling, blissfully unaware of the miserable Christmas dinner on the way.

We're divorced now. It wasn't easy, or cheap. And you are a professor. I hope you continue to enjoy the thrill of late-night yellow-labelled bargains. But think of me in my king-sized bed after a Saturday night out with my new partner, label free.

On the Perilous Edge

I thought I had her but she slipped through my fingers.

Dolly (peroxide curls, Audrey Hepburn headscarf) standing on the cliff top embraces Frank (tweed jacket, Brylcreem, rakish cravat); a clinch to share the grief for a lost daughter.

Hardly.

Dolly leaps backwards, screams and falls to her death on the rocks below. Frank stunned as three whistle-blowing constables bundle him to the ground. They'd seen the couple grappling before Dolly plunged. 'You'll swing for this, me lad,' one says. And he does.

An innocent man hanged? Well…

Earlier, Dolly called the police from the phone box near Beachy Head to say she thought Frank had it in for her.

'And why would he have it in for you madam?'

''Cause he knows I know, 'bout what he did to our Sally, what no man should do to his own daughter. It was in her diary, see, her secret diary. The drugs were just a way out, to escape 'im.'

An open and shut case?

But Frank didn't know she knew. She'd not confronted him but plotted her revenge. So she made the call, walked to the Head, waited for the police to appear, threw her arms around him and then herself off the cliff.

Convincing?

I'm not sure.

Dolly, my tragedienne, can't explain why she would rather Frank hang for her murder than she for his. It would be as easy to push him off as to jump herself – she would welcome death, whether down the cliffs or on the gallows, her loss and anger are unbearable.

Maybe she craved a quick end herself but ignominy for him? That's what I thought but now I'm not sure.

So I'll leave Dolly awhile, floating silently on the perilous edge of a story.

Whose Tomorrow?

After work, crammed into the bar watching it all on the big screen, a man and a woman stand close together. The protest became a riot then a massacre now an uprising. Frantic reporters talk for their lives crouched under pockmarked walls, others behind the front line interview the wounded. One man with blood on his hands tells the camera he's lost his sons. They came to protest peacefully, didn't want trouble, no one did, why did the police open fire, what in God's name was happening, whose blood was this? He doesn't know, shakes his head, wanders away confused.

In the bar, drink flows like there's no tomorrow. The man's wife rings; the city isn't safe, better here in the suburbs, the children are asking how long will he be? Not long.

And the woman's flat-mate too, she can hear gunshots from their balcony, she is frightened, how long will she be? Not long.

An old timer says the President must go, he'd back the rebels. They all would here, but the President is strong, easier said than done, could be a long bloody business, they agree. The army holds the key, which way they go. No love lost between the generals and the President, but the rebels are not their natural allies either. No love lost all round.

The man and woman leave the bar and he takes her hand. It's time, he says. Yes, it is, she replies.

As they approach the train station, the man with blood on his hands walks past, still shaking his head. He glances at them, spits and runs into the night shouting 'Betrayed!'

A distant flash illuminates a skein of smoke rising over the city. She grips his hand tightly, they smile and walk on. This will be their tomorrow.

The Miracle of the Ladder

The miracle is that the ladder is still there, propped securely against the apple tree. Or so it seems. And yet for a second it tipped, I swear it did, tipped just a little, just enough, just as my arm stretched out and I nearly had it in my grasp. Only an apple, of course, but I'd had my eye on it for some time as I harvested the lower branches. It stood out from the rest. Yes, it was a fine looking apple, but no more so than many of the others. Yet it caught my eye and I had to have it, for Françoise.

I'd been warned of course – no climbing ladders, not in my condition, and especially not on my own. But I couldn't resist, it wasn't that high up, I'd only need to climb a few rungs. I'd been climbing that ladder for years and I knew exactly how to secure it, I'd done it so many times. It wasn't like I was trying to repair the roof or anything stupid. No, I was just unlucky. Now, as I lie in the deep grass looking up, I still can't fathom out how the ladder moved. There was no reason for it.

It's dusk and the chill from the dew is creeping through my limbs. Françoise didn't call round after work as she does once or twice a week, to be neighbourly. Francoise is a beauty; blonde hair, bright blue eyes and rosy cheeks. I look forward to her visits even though I know she only comes because my wretched daughter asked her to. But she doesn't seem to mind, she only sees her lover at weekends so maybe she's glad of some company during the week. We drink red wine together on the terrace overlooking the orchard. But she didn't come today and I can't remember if she came yesterday. Things are getting a little blurry.

At least it's not mid-winter, though had it been I wouldn't be picking apples of course. The shivering is getting worse. How can my body summon up the energy to shake violently yet won't allow me to move an inch? Why didn't that ladder budge when I checked it but then tipped just as I was reaching out for my prize? That was Françoise's apple. Now, it's been taken away from me, like everything else. It's too dark to see it but I know it's still up there, hanging over me. When she comes tomorrow I'll point to it and explain that I was picking it for her.

Perhaps she'll see me lying here from her bedroom window before she goes to work. If only I'd cut the grass. If only I hadn't been told no cutting grass with that rusty old mower, no climbing that rickety ladder. I can't even see the top of the ladder anymore. Nothing makes sense. Everything is fading, except her face which glows ever more brightly as the night deepens.

True Blue

Me, a simple working fellow wandering idly through parkland where royal Dukes and their fancy friends have hunted game for centuries. The sun lying low but bright and I swear you could hear the land around bursting into life. There I met a lass by chance, a doe-eyed peasant girl carrying a basket of flowers, stolen no doubt, asked if I was from these parts.

'No, just passing through,' I said, 'an itinerant blacksmith me.'

'Then let me show you round,' she said coyly, 'there's a hunting lodge this way.' And I followed her, of course I did, is my blood not red?

Through grass left wild, down well-trodden paths winding through ancient woods, I followed her tricksy skip until we reached a house ten times bigger than any smithy but a trifling outhouse on this vast estate.

'Is where the masters brought their mistresses, so I've heard,' she teased. 'Still is I reckon,' she whispered, took my rough hand and brazenly opened the door, carelessly left unlocked. Took me up stone stairs to a room with a wide bed heavily laden with furs, air rank with musk, a flagon of wine waiting on a bedside table, rows of slaughtered beasts staring down. She knew this place, was evident even to a simple man. There she spread the stolen flowers across the furs.

I sat next to her on the bed and she stroked my cheek with soft delicate fingers. Too soft for a thief, I reckoned.

'What do I call you?' I asked cunningly.

'Ma'am, if you please,' she said, a twinkle in her true-blue eyes.

'And what do I call you, kind Sir?' she asked demurely.

We lay down, and how we laughed at the thought of our noble forebears and their delicious sports.

Still

Uncle Sam is a legend in the family. Great Great Great Uncle Samuel Bollard, to be precise, lives at the top of our stairs. He's there when I go to bed, sitting serenely on the far left of a quintet of brothers, the youngest and smallest in a line increasing neatly in height and age up to Henry far right, aged twelve. A line of brothers sullen and awkward in their Sunday bests, under bellowed instructions to hold still for the camera until the magnesium powder flashes like a gunshot, their slightly blurred faces attesting to inevitable fright.

Except for Sam, eyes closed as if asleep. Stillest of all, his image is sharp as life compared to his fuzzy siblings; mere sepia ghosts, children long gone, as they would be within a few years. Thomas shot by a sniper on the Somme, Herbert buried in the mud at Ypres, we think, William succumbing to multiple injuries back home in Blighty. Only Henry (my ancestor) survived to marry and have a child, before being taken by influenza.

Yet it's Sam who captivates me, makes me shiver on my way to bed. My grandmother whispered it in my ear one evening as we stood at the top of the stairs. 'Has your father never told you about Uncle Sam?' she cackled gleefully.

Now I know that Sam is not asleep. He succumbed to some childhood ailment just hours before this final portrait of the five Bollard boys. Propped up by a frantic photographer summoned from his home, well paid to create this macabre memento by grieving parents before it was too late. Not uncommon then, grandmother told me. No wonder Sam's siblings were fidgety and downcast.

Now, I can never sneak past that photo without checking Sam's eyes are still closed.

Schrödinger's Other Cat

'The case I have before me…' I quip, to myself (for nobody else is here), '…is an open and shut case.'

The alcohol is kicking in now. I know it is because it's not funny, really, but I'm laughing.

If I was Erwin Schrödinger, there either would or wouldn't be a dead cat in this case. What is it to be? Dead or alive?

I have to face facts, you see, square and fair in the face. I am alone with a case on a remote Danish pier, looking out over the beautiful Øresund, drunk. Sitting on a rickety old wooden pier that used to welcome ferry passengers from Sweden before the majestic Øresund Bridge swept you and your car between Malmo and Copenhagen without blinking an eye. Here I am with a battered leather case, the initials E.S. inscribed in faded gold letters. And I'm toasting it with vodka for the long journey ahead. 'Bon voyage my old friend!' We sit, the case and I, precipitously, on the edge.

Except that I'm not Schrödinger, and there is no cat in this case. In this case, there is something other, possibly.

So why did Schrödinger choose a cat? It could have been anything, sealed up in that box of his (what I call a case because this is *my* case). That is the real mystery, not whether it's dead or not – we've solved that problem – but why a cat? How does physics explain that? Hm? Not in a hurry that's for sure, however fast you accelerate, however near you get to the speed of light.

But this is not *his* case. There is no cat in here, dead or alive. Believe me.

The case is locked. It may not be an open and shut case but I have the key, if I choose to use it. So why not open it and see? Maybe I'd rather not know. At the end of the day – which it is – I miss her.

Whatever's inside, you see, may be dead or alive, and I don't want to know which. Why should I? I'd rather sit on this forgotten pier, enjoying the sounds of the Øresund, the chill air stroking my face, forcing me to breathe in as much as I can consume, washing the vodka down. I may even go for a swim later, as the sun sets. I may dive off this pier into the swirling sea.

One of many possibilities, so many I may drown.

But then there is a creak behind me, a hundred year old wooden beam strains under the weight of a fellow passenger. I turn and there she is – Elena Sundström, smiling.

'I've come for my case,' she says,' I've come to take you home.'

We've come a long way together, Elena and I, so why end it now?

That's my dream, you see. But in the meantime, I rest my case, rest it carefully, just in case. Just in case there is life in it, yet….

Dips

If I were a super-intelligent alien and had a human as a pet, I would feed it dips.

After taking it to the park for a jog, maybe stopping for a cappuccino on the way back, I would sit it down at the kitchen table and take out one of the many trays of dips that I keep, piled up, in my fridge. Sometimes I would give it pitta bread with its dips, lightly toasted, cut into soldiers, and sometimes cool original tortilla chips but not too many. Either way, the plastic tray with four neat compartments would be ideal food for my pet human. Sour cream and chive, tangy salsa, nacho cheese, guacamole – what a lucky human!

Once it had eaten, and enjoyed a soapy bath, I would give my human its remote control to play with. I know how much it would enjoy flicking between channels, apparently at random, dipping in and out, until eventually it would tire of it all, the flicking and flickering would stop, and it would be time for bed. How sweet it would look curled up, grasping its favourite blanket, to sleep perchance to dream of dips.

And although I was super-intelligent, I wouldn't recognise human speech so I couldn't understand it when it said, quietly but firmly, looking up at me with those doleful eyes, 'I don't want any more dips,' and so I would keep on feeding it dips, day after day after day.

After all, humans deserve their dips.

The Second One

'It's always the second pint that tastes the best, no matter how many you have.' And Liam usually had way more.

'The hit from the first kicks in, anticipation grows, that hard-earned thirst still waits to be quenched,' he enthused. 'Anything seems possible. It's a pivotal moment; the first downed abruptly, no more than a primer really, the second waiting to be relished.'

The only spoiler, as Liam knows, it that it won't last, can't last. The second will be consumed, and then it'll be the third, and the fourth most likely. Driven by the law of diminishing returns, he will carry on, long into another hazy, fragmented night.

He told Debbie this as they thought about what next, the day they walked hand-in-hand along the towpath near the town where he was born, thirty years and three children ago. Debbie thought the canal smelled rank but didn't say anything; they were too caught up in each other, sharing dreams that were eagerly forming into plans.

'I only drink when I'm unhappy', Liam explained, 'and I'm happy with you'.

And he was, and so was she with him, so much so they broke their vows to others and made new ones. Our 'second life' they called it. When they moved in together,

Debbie made it a rule that he could have no more than two pints in an evening. They laughed like they'd forgotten how to.

But she was rarely there when he sank the first.

The Price of a Normal life

While we wait for Ziggy to return with the ransom money, Albi passes the time with a confession. Hood removed, I see we are in some sort of church hall, dimly lit and musty.

'I have this recurring nightmare that I'm asleep,' he says confusingly, 'dreaming that I'm living a normal sort of life, but then suddenly I wake up and realise that I've been asleep at the wheel of my car and I'm driving fast along a motorway, but it's too late to do anything about it. The car's out of control. It's all over.'

Albi looks sad, resigned. The gag stuffed into my mouth stops me replying, or warning him. Ziggy, suitcase in one hand, gun in the other, fires through the back of Albi's head and his body slumps to the floor at my feet.

I look up and notice a sign above Ziggy's head instructing us to 'stack all chairs and tables away after use.'

'No point sharing,' says Ziggy smiling, then points the gun at me, 'no point handing you back neither, not now I've got what I want.'

Tied to the chair, I can't move. I close my eyes as he pulls the trigger.

Then I wake up and I'm driving fast along a motorway.

It's night time, lights flash past and straight towards me. It's too late, I'm out of control.

This is my normal life. How much is it worth? How much is there in that suitcase, Ziggy?

Aftermath

Next day, first light, we emerge from the clouds. Tom, flying beside me, points to our village way below, lying ruined on the cliffs. We descend slowly, hesitantly, the wind buffeting us with the last spasms of the gale that broke open our walls in the night, sending us spinning into the sea.

Tom is the first to notice bodies strewn across the rocks. He looks at me, but I can't see clearly from this height to offer any comfort.

'Let's go down,' I shout, and he and the others nod solemnly.

We swoop back and fro over the rubble, but there is no sign of life. Waves still crash on the rocks, but these are not the monsters that took our wives and children before we'd a chance to say farewell. More than two dozen souls perished, and then there was us. We have to land if we can, there is work to do. We owe them that at least.

But our wings are fledgling, our control clumsy, and there is little flat ground left to receive us. The stone houses had always perched uneasily on the steep cliffs above the beach where we kept our boats; a tight community of fisher folk, feeding off the sea, living on the edge, some of us depending too much on piety for our salvation.

A few undignified flaps and we tumble onto a small cobbled space where only yesterday we'd sewed nets and fretted about the stormy air. We begin the unhappy salvage that last night we prayed would be a rescue. Tom walks ahead with the others but I hesitate, my vision blurred, eyes stinging and shoulders aching from the weight of fresh wings.

Too late, I begin to understand the dismal burden of angels.

The Chosen One

It was hard to believe the honour and good fortune bestowed on me. A young stonemason from a mountain village, chosen by the High Priest for the most coveted duty in the land. From dozens of hopeful, desperate men paraded before his beady eye that day, I was the one picked as worthy of the Queen's pleasure.

Before my appointment, a handmaiden oiled my body with almond balm, including my manhood which, she said, had to be primed for the heady task ahead.

'Spill your seed in her and your entire family will be fed to the pigs,' she warned.

It would be wise, she counselled, to make use of her attentions to 'empty myself', to help me in meeting the Queen's decree. The handmaiden was brisk and efficient and hid the evidence ingeniously.

Dressed in purple robes, I was taken to the Queen's dimly-lit chamber and announced by the High Priest, who then withdrew, head lowered, shuffling backwards while she remained barely visible in the shadows.

I was nervous but tried not to shake as she told me to disrobe and lie on the enormous bed covered in sumptuous silks of every hue, steeped in the pungent fragrance of myrrh. Only then did she appear, our divine matriarch, not dressed as I had imagined in majestic splendour, but in a simple cotton gown, her long grey hair loose, like a mere woman.

I had lain with village girls, all shiny skin and proud breasts, but those were frantic, opportunistic couplings. This was our sacred Queen and my family's honour was at stake. They said she was a hundred, which I doubt, but it was not a firm maiden's body and I quickly worried I would prove an unworthy choice.

My doubts soon vanished. While others, even the High Priest, dare not catch her eye, I was enticed into the greatest of intimacies that I cannot describe, suffice to say she was highly skilled in the arts of lovemaking and knew every ruse to keep me strong. My father can take pride from my endurance.

Despite her guile, her varied and seemingly endless desires, I spilled not a drop of my seed, not even when her short sharp gasps rose into a she-wolf's cry that must have been heard throughout the palace.

Falling limply onto the bed beside me, she told me simply to 'go'.

My purpose fulfilled, I dressed and walked to the door, looking proudly ahead, never back. There had been many before, and would be many after, but that was my night, my moment.

As the chamber door closed behind, guards standing on either side grabbed my shoulders and pushed my head down onto a block. A third guard, wielding an axe, completed the ritual.

It seemed a small price to pay for the privilege of being the chosen one for a night. My family's standing would rise in our village, throughout the mountains, and I would be remembered as a hero, touched by immortality.

A Bigger Heavier Thing

It felt heavier than I was used to, and bigger, but the nice man with the beard showed me what to do with it. He let me try it on a sack of grain. It was quite hard to keep hold of it, keep it steady and the noise was deafening at first. But I got used to it after a few goes. There was grain everywhere. He said I could take home a sack later to my parents, as a reward, if I was good.

Then the man with the beard led me into this courtyard that was very hot and told me to stand still and do exactly what he told me to do. Another man, without a beard, was filming him with his camera and the man with a beard was shouting loudly and waving his arms about like he was really angry.

I didn't notice the blond haired man at first as he was crouched over in the corner of the courtyard with his back to me. He was very quiet. The bearded man led me over towards him and the man with the camera followed us. The man with the beard said some more things into the camera and then nodded to me. I did what I'd been taught. It was easy.

After that they told me to go away – not even a bag of grain even though I'd done what I was supposed to do, and done it properly. So I went back to the street to play with my friends. I got bored after a while though. It wasn't fair, they wouldn't fall over if I shot them, and even when they did, they got back up again and started firing at me. That's not how it is.

Red Fluff

In the morning, there is scant to see. Just some empty glasses, exhausted candles, torn clothes strewn like pelts, a cruel belt hanging from the bed post, those tiny bits of tell-tale fluff, red against the stained white sheet. And the delicious scent of our secrets.

I lie and listen to your body cleansing.

But then you're clean gone, the air is clear, wine stains wiped softly down the sink, remnants of our scratched skins binned, clawed to dust by lovers just a flinch from fear. Only the red fluff remains, spilt from cuffs, scattered like the lost feathers of a startled bird.

Later, I slumber, still alone, pure as the dull dripping clock, lying on a memory speckled white, of a flickering fight by candle-light. Left to recall the thrall in your wide and frightened eyes, I brush the love fluff from my sheet – it resists, naturally, defiant and indelible.

Tomorrow, you will come again, disturb my gravitas with your Shiraz, be wanton with my wax, dangling your fetters like garlands. We will entwine, decorate our flesh, worry the sweat from our glands, wallow in a dark and desperate place.

Yet you cleanse yourself so easily.

One day, the fluff will take flight, sucked into a mass of debris, and at last there will be time to retreat, to wonder where else you prowl and prey through foul and fertile nights.

Then I will walk slowly, sober, to the shower and burn my skin as raw as silk.

Enduring, with Gentle Bitterness

Ebullient indeed, Grace thinks from the back of the hall. The slip of paper reads, 'your ebullient host for this evening's tasting is Keith McKinnon, ambassador with the Scotch Malt Whisky Society.'

Keith exudes enthusiasm, half-moon glasses resting on his red nose as he swirls the golden liquid before dipping into the glass and inhaling deeply.

'I'm getting the sweetness of vanilla, Coco pops, baked lemon cheesecake and Play-Doh,' he intonates with that sonorous voice redolent of their days treading the boards, he the dashing leading man, she the faithful chorus girl. The voice still enthralls, its huskiness thickened by smoke and spirit.

He sips, glares pensively at the expectant audience.

'Mm,' he teases, 'a subtle blend of sweetness and bitterness, reminiscent of cherry brandy, uncooked buttery pastry and chamois leather.'

The crowd, a dozen or so dusty Rotary Club locals, mimic his moves, sniffing and sipping in unison, desperate to share his sensitive palate, torn between admiration and bafflement.

He adds a drop of water and sips again.

'Ah,' he wheezes, 'now there's citrus, fruity toffee, nut brittle and lolly sticks.'

A few concur with knowing nods, others sip again, frustrated by inadequate taste buds.

'And finally,' he drools, 'hints of menthol and yacht varnish in the after-taste.'

He swallows the residue, holds the glass to the light and concludes; 'Overall, an enduring perfume with a hint of gentle bitterness. Jolly good value, I'd say.'

At the evening's hazy end, bottles are bought recklessly from Grace's table while Keith collects glasses and downs the scraps. The Rotarians totter home to share a few slurred pearls with waiting wives;

'…a drop of water brings out a whole raft of different flavours…',

'…it's the barrel that gives whisky its colour…',

'…once whisky is bottled it stops maturing, so you might as well drink it…'.

Worth the ticket price alone, they think.

The takings, after costs, are barely enough to pay for the B&B where Keith rests his head on Grace's plump bosom while she strokes the threadbare scalp that once boasted a thick dark mop, reminiscent of Cary Grant she thought. Her career dissolved when he asked her to be his leading lady, the only role she ever coveted. Still does, even as she lies awake fretting through the long guttural snores.

When roused, he will be raring for a Full English, while she skips the saturates to plan the next tasting in the next town. As she drives, he will smoke his way through the Daily Mail muttering about a world gone mad. Booked into the next B&B, he heads for a bar in preparation for another ebullient performance. She watches old films on TV. They will meet at the venue, some old hall, cold and rarely used, and carry boxes of whisky and glasses together from the rusty Morris Traveller. Breathless, he will consult again the Society's notes about each of the single malts and rehearse his lines.

It's a travelling show she knows can't splutter on forever.

Enough to Wake the Dead

It's the alarm clocks that keep me awake. Not mine, I don't need one, but others in the street; next door, a few doors away, somewhere in the distance, but always there, always ringing.

Just alarm clocks. No voices, shouts to get out of bed, toilets flushing, showers running, stairs descended, front doors slamming, cars starting, cars passing. None of that, just the alarm clocks ringing. It's enough…

No snoozing, not now. Pushing the curtain aside, I see the fog has not yet lifted, maybe never will. No point in getting up I suppose but I can't shake the habit. Can't sleep with all these alarms going off so I go downstairs, quietly so as not to wake…

Make myself a cup of tea, black of course, no milkman these days. No clinking of bottles or the stop-start whir of the milk float, the squeaky brakes. I miss those sounds. But you can get used to black tea, I find, if you need to.

Today is my birthday and I try to make the most of it, open a new packet of biscuits – still a few left though they're hard to bite into now – add a drop of whisky to my tea. I would have finished the whisky ages ago except I don't like the stuff. Tastes OK in tea though, a bit special.

The radio is a comfort. No more news, just gentle music, the occasional voice of a presenter calmly introducing the next piece. 'And now something from the repertoire of that master of Baroque…' Good to know they're out there somewhere playing music, still.

I wouldn't mind so much if it wasn't for the alarms ringing all through the night. And it's never daylight anymore.

Surely that's enough now? Enough to…

Enough, please.

Once

Yesterday, on a busy street in the city, out of the corner of my eye I glimpsed a woman I once loved. I didn't catch her eye but simply walked past like I hadn't noticed her. But I could tell she had seen me and was thinking that I would see her, and we would stop and greet each other like long lost lovers, or old friends at least.

But I chose not to, I just walked on past and the moment was lost, the chance to catch up after years, for no reason other than we had met, by chance, on a busy street, miles from both our houses, where we live comfortably with our partners and children.

But that's not the issue, now or then. We first met by chance but became lovers through desire. It was that simple. That was our time, our place, and this isn't. It's not that we are married or have children. We could have been friends then but we chose not to be, so why now?

As I walked away, sensing a slight hesitation in her stride, I knew I was leaving something behind, something that her unseen glance wanted to retain, or at least acknowledge. Not desire, not now, but a claim to something that once lived which only we shared. Like the child we never had, never could have.

There was no sound as we moved apart. No 'hi' that would have been impossible to ignore. Maybe she also knew that unless our eyes met there was the possibility that we could pass by each other as if nothing had ever happened.

This is an absence I can accept, and I hope she can. A moment that might have been, once, but now melts into the anonymity of a crowd.

Charming and Naïve

Charming and naïve, these paintings of fruit, birds, feathers, seashells. Stacked up in the studio-shed, they await the journey to the gallery, to be hung and smiled at, maybe even bought by city folk on weekend trips to the seaside. But for now they sit in line, alongside unfinished others while the artist lies in her bath in the plum orchard nearby, eagerly anticipating the appearance of stars.

The water is heated by hot coals laid carefully beneath the old tub, held up by stones. Her dress hangs limply on branches some distance away to avoid the steam as it rises and dissolves in darkness. She has endured the moment of pain, the transition from stark chilly nakedness as she takes off her sandals and climbs into the bath to immerse herself in almost unbearable heat, forcing a breathless stupor until her inner body adapts and the heat gradually begins to dissipate. She knows it is a necessary pain, necessary to achieve blissful equilibrium when she can breathe again, sip whisky and gaze up at the baffling array of twinkling lights scattered above her, above everyone that has ever lived.

She thinks about the paintings that are leaving, those not yet ready and those yet to be born, her gifts of sorts to people she'll probably never meet – services to strangers is how she thinks of it. All she asks in return is the means to carry on.

Later, she hears the crack of a fallen branch and knows it's time to brave the sharp cold again before it consumes her by stealth. He emerges from the cottage, as always at this time, instinctively. He watches her rise up, step out and tiptoe, shivering, to collect her towel from him, dry herself briskly and slip on her dress and sandals. He's here to play his part, to kick away the coals so they don't crack the bath, and carry her back in his arms through the orchard to the cottage.

As they pass her shed tonight, she wonders who this man really is, this man who silently indulges her penchant for night-baths in the orchard, who surely shares the same view of the stars? Is he a fallen angel perhaps or some Aztec priest carrying her to the altar?

'I think I'll paint some more,' she says, so he carries her into her shed and lays her on the small bed that she uses to avoid disturbing him when she works late, as she often does. She has a kettle there, spare clothes, whisky, chocolate to keep her going, a fire if needed. He kisses her and smiles, and closes the shed door quietly behind him as if she were asleep already.

She lies on the bed for a while looking at an unfinished painting of yellow quinces in a blue bowl that sits expectantly on her easel. If, one day, a stranger recognises the charm and naïvety of it, she won't be disappointed.

The Day That Happened

The day began with a trip to the park with Tove, his granddaughter. Her mother dropped her off on the way to work and, as it was already sunny, they decided to go straightaway. Tove was familiar with the playground from previous visits.

'Higher, higher,' she screamed on the swings, 'faster, faster,' on the roundabout.

'What's the rush?' he said, 'we've got all day.' How long was all day to a child, he wondered. Forever probably.

After lunch it rained so they played 'Concentration'. Tove lost the first game and sulked. She didn't want to play again but then she couldn't think of anything else she'd like to do, so they did. This time she won (he let her) which cheered her up so they played a third and she won again (this time for real).

'You're getting too good for me,' he said.

'I know,' Tove said, and smiled.

They made some lemonade together, with real lemons, but it was too sharp for Tove so she had Coke instead. He thought it was too sharp as well but still drank it. 'Mm, delicious,' he said. He watched her suck the last few noisy drops of Coke from her glass.

'Have I told you about the time your mother made me cry?' he asked. 'She was about your age. We'd been for a picnic by the river, your grandma and me, your mother and Uncle Jens. We'd had a lovely day but on the way back, she stopped, looked at me crossly and said…'

'Why do days have to end? Why can't they just go on and on? Yes, you told me before grandpa'.

'Did I? Sorry, I don't remember.'

After that Tove was happy to play by herself until it was time to go. When her mother arrived he invited them to stay for tea, but no they had to get back, things to do, but thanks, thanks for everything.

He was sad to see them go but knew that he'd see them again soon, not like his other grandchildren, what were their names? He'd seen less and less of them since he'd been living alone.

In the evening he made himself an omelette and printed some of the photos of Tove he'd taken that day, to remind him. He pinned them carefully onto his notice board on top of ones taken last time she came. Such days are tiring but precious, he thought.

The sky had cleared again so he sat in the garden with a bottle of Lakka and toasted the stars as they appeared; a sip for each, a glass for every constellation. Alone, he glided slowly but surely through the night until it grew too cold and he knew he had to move while he still could. He sloped into bed and slipped into dreams he would never remember, before waking, a little more befuddled than yesterday – a day that had been higher and faster than ever, he thought, another day that had happened.

A Lifetime

We were allowed outside for the eclipse.

'Ten minutes, only,' Mr Pomphrey warned, already reaching for his Woodbines.

'I'm not fussed,' Cerys confided to me, 'but better than bloody maths.'

'There won't be another one in our lifetime,' I told her, 'not a total, solar one.'

'Really?' she gasped, those clear green eyes alive with interest, inviting me to continue. My heart thumped.

'Be eighty years before this happens again. The moon passing across the sun so it blocks it out completely. Right here in the valley.'

She looked up at the sky, squinting.

'But you mustn't look, you'll damage your eyes.'

Those perfect eyes.

'What's the point then? What's the point if you can't see it?' She turned away.

'It'll go dark,' I said drawing her back, 'very soon, you see, eerily gloomy for a few minutes and silent, deathly silent. Birds will fall from the sky.'

Her eyes widened again.

'Really?' she said, and grabbed my hand.

In the playground the other children ran around frantically while we waited, hand in hand. Then it clouded over. But even the extra gloom was barely noticeable. Children laughed and dogs barked. No birds fell from the sky. Mr Pomphrey appeared.

'OK you lot, back inside, party's over.'

'Dai's got a new catapult,' she told me, pulling away, 'promised he'd show it me after school.' She didn't look back.

A lifetime later, Cerys' green eyes are alive with wonder again, surely for the last time, shining plain in that long lost valley.

Justin Kershaw: A Life in Books

For sale, the complete works of Justin Kershaw (first editions signed by the author), comprising:

'Corn Ears in the Breeze' (1959) – his international best-seller, a vivid semi-autobiographical portrait of childhood on the idyllic North Yorkshire moors in the 1930s, growing up amid a cast of colourful relatives and hilariously eccentric locals.

'A sparkling debut from a major new talent. I defy any reader not to be captivated by Kershaw. A breath of fresh Yorkshire air.'

'Maleficence in Morden' (1970) – Justin's long-awaited second novel takes an existential view of post-war Britain through the eyes of a successful author haunted by his past.

'An unexpectedly heavyweight, intense tome from the author of the much-loved "Corn Ears in the Breeze" in which Kershaw swops the enchanting landscapes of the moors for the hard-edged urban streets of London. Not an easy read.'

'More Ears in the Breeze' (1979) – twenty years on, the widely-welcomed follow-up to 'Corn Ears in the Breeze' picks up Justin's story at university in the 1940s and his early days as a struggling writer in London.

'For lovers of his debut novel who demanded more, this is certainly it.'

'Before Ears' (1999) – Justin's autobiography published shortly before his death tells the harrowing story of his upbringing, his drunken and abusive father and the awful dreariness of life in pre-war Yorkshire.

'Not for the faint hearted, this swingeing portrait of rural depravity and family misery will shock lovers of his early writing. Not so much setting the record straight as throwing it away and starting again.'

'Corn Ears in the Breeze' (2009, 50th anniversary edition) –

"A deserved celebration of this 20th century classic that captures forever an almost forgotten world of family togetherness and rural bliss. No coming-of-age novel so deserves its place in the canon.' Not signed.

Paris No Sale

That's what it reads on the till register, in stark digital letters. There for all to see, like Paris herself; brazen yet sullen.

I reflect, as I sip my flat white, careful not to disturb the perfectly formed fern leaf she carefully and skilfully crafted. It has to go, of course, but I want to make it last as long as possible. It would be disrespectful not to, I believe. I do it for her, for Paris. After all, like me, she is an artiste.

Paris wipes glasses and places them carefully on the bar. Then she turns, looks at herself in the mirror and distractedly strokes the blonde bun tied up above her nape. She glances at me for a moment. I look away. Does she wonder why I choose to sit at the bar, on this uncomfortable stool, when there are tables available with more space to work? No, Paris No Sale has other things on her mind. Coffee to make, fern leaves to craft, artistry to perform.

Why 'No Sale'? She is a meticulous worker, whether handling glasses or decorating coffee. She may not have made a sale, it seems, but she is deft, light on her feet, not friendly but efficient, professional. She serves me, and all customers, despite the denial on the till. It's hard to capture this in charcoal. I have my limitations.

And what does this beauty think of the hazy figure sitting along the bar, sketching silently? Not much, I'm sure. Paris No Sale, always serving but never selling, gazes mournfully away from me, at customers yet to appear.

But in some other dimension, from another perspective, in some future painting, I gaze into her eyes, and she mine.

After Edouard Manet's 'A Bar at the Folies-Bergère'

After the Fall

A few weeks after the fall of Troy I got a job there as a chippy. Times were tough in our village, the Greeks had passed through and not touched a thing, nothing to repair – I was gutted. But I figured there would be work going in Troy, plenty of re-building and refurbishment, what with the sacking and all. So I packed my tools, gave the old woman a slap to remind her, and walked the fifty or so miles along the slopes of Mount Ida.

Sure enough, there was no shortage of work, though not a lot of cash, so I worked for food and somewhere to sleep mostly, and a few promises which were rarely kept. I began to build a reputation for being one of the more reliable and, generally, sober workers. I also had all my limbs intact, an advantage over most of the local tradesmen it seemed, so much so that I was chosen to take on a really important job.

This official-looking guy said there was a structure that needed breaking up, so he took me round the back of one of the temples into a yard near the main gate and there it was, this enormous wooden horse. No kidding!

'Why d'you want it broken up?' I asked.

'What else are we going to do with it, you twat? Not going to get used again, is it?' he said.

'I'll take it off your hands,' I said, 'how much do you want?'

A lot more than I had of course. But I said I would get the cash somehow, work day and night, don't you worry. You could tell he thought I was a bit mad but when I said where I was from, he just nodded and smiled; he obviously knew that men from my village were men of their word.

It was clear that the odd bit of carpentry wouldn't be enough, so I went to the posh houses and offered my services, in whatever capacity they needed. Invariably it was the lady of the house who was in need of my assistance, what with all the recent male mortality. Typically this involved repairs to their damaged property but then I managed to boost my takings by providing more personal services, shall we say. They seem satisfied with my efforts and often recommended me to friends. Sometimes they would club together and get me to do a job lot which I thought was a bit cheap but I was in no position to complain. It was hard to get cash but often they would pay me with decent trinkets that I could sell in the market.

Eventually I got the money together but by the time I went back, the horse had already been dismantled. The official-looking guy said he didn't think I was coming back, someone else had got the job and now it was just a pile of wood sitting there waiting to be sold. Several piles in fact.

'I'll buy the lot,' I said, and he laughed again.

But I did. He wanted a small fortune, compared with what I'd been offered to break it up. I haggled him down and paid half up front, which took all the money I had, but I told him I'd be back later with the rest, no problem. He took me at my word this time, he knew I was reliable and hard-working, word had got round.

So I worked some more for the good ladies of Troy – it wasn't easy but I kept it up – and then went back to pay the rest. I think he was just glad to get rid of it in the end, those piles of wood had been clogging up the yard for weeks. He seemed pleased to see it go anyway, quite a party turned up, cheered me all the way to the gate.

I made sure I had enough money for some donkeys and a string of carts to take the wood back to my village. It was hard going but we made it in the end. Caused a bit of a stir, I can tell you, back in the village. The old woman was impressed, you can imagine, me turning up with a dozen cart loads of pre-loved wood and not a penny to my name.

'What the fuck are you going to do with that lot?' she asked politely.

'I'm going to build me a wooden horse,' I said, just to wind her up.

I meant it though, of course. She'd not heard much about the fall of Troy, how it had actually happened and all. So I told her the story, although she still couldn't get her head round what I was up to.

'Fucking barking', she said. She never did appreciate my spark of genius.

There were one or two complaints from the neighbours about the mess and the noise, but nothing the gift of a serviceable donkey wouldn't settle. So I rebuilt the wooden horse, bit by bit, day after day, week after week, until it was back to its original glory, just as it must have been when it was first built, near enough.

Then I waited. By that time the old woman had long gone but more fool her I thought. She didn't have my foresight, you see, she didn't know what I knew – that the wooden horse of Troy would become one of the greatest legends of our civilisation.

And so I waited. I sat quietly on the edge of the village, laughing with the children who were sent along to play with me and my horse, keep me entertained while I waited, safe in the knowledge that it wouldn't be long before some really rich geezer would turn up and offer me a vast fortune for this famous, fabulous relic, this iconic memento of the fall of Troy.

One day we will all be laughing together.

One day soon…

Fortune

A memorable Christmas thanks to our Berni's good fortune and generosity.

Lavish gifts all round – widescreen plasma TV for Mam, MacBook for me, an iPhone for little Finn. Barely able to hold it, Finn treated it as the toy it was, in effect. I took my MacBook to bed and stroked it.

'You're too generous, Berni,' Mam said, 'I can't believe you found all these things in the sales!'

'They start early these days, Mam,' said Berni.

'Even so, how could you afford all this?'

'Being in the right place at the right time. Good fortune.'

'Fortune is what the dear Lord bestows on the righteous,' said Mam, 'it was meant to be.'

'Fortune is as fortune does,' said Berni. She gave me that big sister shrug with the blank but loaded look. I responded with my equally blank yet rebellious kid sister stare.

'That's what your Da, God rest his soul, used to say, and it came back to bite him alright,' said Mam.

Our misfortunate father, lost at sea it seemed. And why not? It's not uncommon round here.

Berni's good fortune was toasted with sherry as we watched highlights of the year's news on the supersized screen. Hazy CCTV footage of someone in a hoodie, scarf wrapped round their face, helping themselves from a branch of Comet at the height of the summer's riots. I swished the sweet liquid around my mouth, making it last as long as I could.

'Terrible what some kids get up to,' Mam said, 'what their poor parents must think!'

She looked up at our Saviour gazing down benignly from his perch above the fireplace, tarnished gold tinsel draped around his frame.

'How blessed I am,' she said, taking another sip.

'True enough, Mam,' said Berni, who turned to me and winked.

The Name

They were in the café where they had first met three years before. He suggested going there. She thought it was as good a place as any, it didn't really matter to her.

'If I write a name on a piece of paper, you have to tell me what it is,' he said.

She looked at him pityingly.

'Why?'

'I need to know you can do it.'

'But why?'

'I just do. I can't explain.'

Pity edged towards exasperation.

'But of course I can't. How could I?'

'Just do it. You can do it, I know you can.'

'What's the point?'

That pained expression again, his favourite.

'It's something to do with us. Something we can do, together.'

'But isn't that the point? We're not together, not any more. That's why we're here, talking about our future, or lack of it. And even if we were still together, what is the chance of me guessing some random name on a piece of paper?'

'No, that would be the point. It wouldn't be random, it would be meaningful, a name we have in common, one we both know.'

'This is ridiculous. We're supposed to be discussing the future and you want to play stupid games. Maybe that sums it all up.'

'It's not a stupid game. It has a purpose, it means everything.'

She was used to his melodrama. He wouldn't be satisfied until…

'OK, OK, let's do it. Let's see what it really means. Go on, write it down, write down the name. And then maybe we can get on with the rest of our lives.'

Two can play this game.

He wrote down the name on a piece of paper, without hesitation.

'OK.'

She looked at his face, that familiar anxious face, knowing the chances of getting it right were slim verging on zero. Nothing in their current, fragile and deteriorating relationship provided any sort of clue to the name he had written down. If she got it wrong, which surely she would, it proved nothing. And even if, by some miracle, she got it right, it wouldn't prove anything either, not to her anyway, although she knew he would interpret it in his own inimitable way.

She wanted to be wrong, of course, and although every bit of common sense told her to say something, anything, any name she could think of, just so her life could begin again, she didn't. She sat and stared at him, his eager eyes and restless mouth, and waited, paralysed by indecision. She waited and waited, turning names over in her mind, over and over but never totally sure, never sure enough to say anything. Until eventually he turned over the piece of paper.

LAKATOS

It wasn't even a name she had ever heard of. It meant nothing to her.

'You had your chance,' he said, smiling, knowing she would never have got it right.

'I know,' she said, smiling too, knowing he could never do that to her again.

Eye for I

Lying in the bath, the night after Anna left, he thought long and hard about the title.

'*Looking through Lana Del Rey's Eyes*' he liked for its rhythm, but it wasn't particularly relevant; some might be disappointed when they realised it had little to do with the surly singer.

'*Cross Eyed Girls Are Easy*' had a nice ring to it but might be considered cruel. He didn't want to offend anyone, not even Anna, really.

The other front runner was '*I Don't Want to Even Go There!*' Anna's last words to him reflected his central theme of 'avoidance' but was maybe a bit too Carveresque?

The clichéd '*Elephant in the Room*' was another contender, briefly.

'*Why don't you want to have sex with me anymore?*' was to the point but lacked the subtlety deserving of his carefully wrought prose, he felt. Besides, it wasn't really about that. It was about how she kept tripping over things and stopped watching TV. How she didn't want to talk about it, just shout a lot, and drink a lot, and trip over some more.

As the bathwater cooled and *her* soapsuds fizzled into nothing, and *her* candle wicks sank further into their self-made holes, he still couldn't decide. So he pulled the plug, lay back and let the water drain around him. A ghostly draft left him in total darkness. Gravity returned with a vengeance as the bath emptied, squashing his suddenly heavy limbs against the hard sides of a ceramic coffin. He wasn't sure he even had the strength to get out.

The story was published posthumously under the title he finally chose shortly before the end, '*Eye*'. By then Anna was blind and could only listen to it on audio. She thought it a fitting title. 'It was always about him.'

Janey's Book of Many Faces

O Janey, my prodigal daughter. I pop in most days to check she's OK, catch up on her news, what's she's been up to. I don't say much unless I feel I need to. But sometimes I do, of course I do.

'Sarah-Jane,' I say, 'what are you doing?'

She doesn't reply for ages.

'Go away. Keep out of it.'

'But Janey, he's not your type. Look at him. Unkempt, scrawny – he's not on drugs is he? And whatever is he wearing? He looks like a clown.'

'It's a fancy dress party.'

'Why's he leering at you like that? Where's his other hand?'

'He's just a friend.'

'A friend? I hate to think… What's he studying?'

'Games technology.'

'What sort of subject is that? If only you'd gone to a proper university. If only you'd tried a bit harder at school. He's got a beard for God's sake, he must be on drugs.'

She doesn't reply. She often goes quiet like this, it's infuriating. She treats me like I'm not really there, like I'm just another face in her book of many faces. I'll talk to her when she comes home.

'Let's catch up soon,' I say. No more questions, no need to answer, not now.

I'll pop in again tomorrow, check she's OK. I won't say anything, as long as she's OK, as long as I don't need to. I'll wait until she comes home. She must come home soon, surely? She can't ignore her father forever.

How I Acquired a Decent Suit

Anyway, as I told the police, I found this feller face down (well, what was left of his face) at the bottom of the gorge. Jumped from the viewing platform I reckon, they usually do. Thought about it myself once or twice to be honest but this feller put me off for life I can tell you. Had my share of bad luck you see, so I reckoned I deserved a break; you can't blame me for having a quick peek in his wallet, can you? Told the police I was just seeing if he had any ID, to explain why my grubby prints were all over it. OK, I admit I helped myself to a few notes, left some behind as well of course, but why would anyone care? And then there was this dry cleaning ticket. Thing is, he looked about my size, from what I could tell, well dressed, and I needed a new suit or coat or whatever. After all, he wasn't going to need it anymore was he? No one would know. No one would care.

He had a mobile in his pocket so I gave the police a call and they came and sorted him out. I waited there with him 'till they arrived, not that he was going anywhere. Came to interview me later, the police that is, as they do, so I told them about how I came across the poor sod while I was out walking, minding my own business, the shock of it all, terrible business etc. They seemed to accept that I wasn't some sort of psycho, just a regular harmless sort of guy, which is true.

Looked like a straightforward case to them I reckon. No obvious funny business, just another crumpled body at the bottom of the gorge. He lived alone they said, this guy, no relatives as far as they could tell. Said his flat was a complete tip when they went to look, stuff thrown about everywhere, helluva mess. No sign of a break-in. Must have gone off his rocker for some reason, they reckoned, poor bastard.

So that's how I acquired a decent suit. Three piece, tweed job too, good condition, snug fit, and nice and clean of course. He hadn't paid for the dry cleaning up front but I can hardly complain really, can I?

Oh yes, I nearly forgot. In the suit pocket I found another ticket. Not a dry cleaning one, but a lottery ticket, Euro Lottery to be precise. So I thought I'd check it out and you'll never guess, he'd only gone and won bloody Euromillions!

Poor bugger, just think, he could be standing here now holding this giant cheque with one hand, glass of champagne in the other, smiling at the camera, wearing this nice clean suit. He must have dreamt of this moment when his numbers came up. If only he'd remembered where he'd left his ticket.

Post, Nail, Thieves…?

Sully, 'dumb as a post', our Dad would say. He was a matter-of-fact man, said it as it was.

Couldn't speak a word, Sully, but not for lack of trying. No lack of noise neither, plenty of grunts but not a word known to man.

Sully got by.

'A careful grunt's better than a torrent of badly chosen words,' Mum would say, and smile with the truth of it.

No lack of brains neither, it turns out, reading and writing no problem. Words flowed, and numbers galore, all correctly accounted for too.

'Dumb as a post, sharp as a nail,' Dad would say, and smile with the truth of it.

Got into numbers big, computer programming and all that. 'A whizz', everyone agreed. Doing stuff we had no idea about. Not even his teachers could keep up.

'Nothing more we can do for him,' they said, like he was some lost cause.

Spent most days in his room after that, talking to folk all over the world. We called it talking anyway, good as. Had friends in countries I'd never heard of. Made a real friend too, best friend, guy called Jude who'd come round daily and disappear into Sully's room. Jude wouldn't say much either, but wasn't dumb. 'Thick as thieves,' Dad would say.

Until they came one night, took Sully away, silently, like they knew he had nothing to say in his defence.

Found him nailed up in the square next day like a common thief. No sign of Jude. Example to us all not to meddle, they said. Extinction the only way forward for mutants, they said.

'Sully's dead,' Dad said, 'dead as a –.'

'No!' Mum said, 'He's still out there, talking away to everyone, I know he is, and that's the Truth of it.'

At The End of the Day

So I told her, I said, you know I like to watch the footie in the evening, especially if United are playing. She won't let me have Sky, you see, not until she can have a new cooker, she says, so now Five Live is on the telly it's a chance to enjoy some live matches. Put me feet up, glass or two of black magic, bit of cheese and biscuits at half time, it's a good way to unwind, especially if we've been bowling.

Joan reckons it's sad, watching Five Live on the telly. Why don't you go upstairs and listen to it on the radio, she says, then I can watch summat else in the front room. But I'm watching the footie, I tell her, it's United tonight, I like to watch it on the big screen, you know I do. I know it only says 'you are listening to Five Live' but that's not the point. it's your turn tomorrow, I tell her. I don't think that's unreasonable, do you?

And you've gotta have the build-up, savour the atmosphere. It's all about the anticipation, I tell her, but she doesn't get it. Why can't I watch Emmerdale, she says, match doesn't start until eight. She doesn't get that anticipation is everything, when anything is still possible.

She likes a good moan, our Joan, always get an earful when she wakes me up. I know the match hasn't always finished but it's all but over, obvious how it's going to finish, just waiting for the fat lady to sing, or moan.

Anyway, I'm not asleep, I tell her, just listening with me eyes closed.

Can't stand all that chit chat after though, complaining about the referee, all the ifs and buts, how it might have all been so different, if only. Go on and on about it. What's the point? It's over, done with, nothing's going to change. After all, it's only a game. At least that's something we agree on, me and Joan. At the end of the day, that's all it is.

Making do

15.25 I'll get wasabi nuts if you get prosecco.

15.33 Got wasabi nuts. OK for prosecco?

15.46 Got prosecco just in case.

16.26 Forgot coriander, can you cover?

17.41 How's it going? Started cooking.

18.07 Where are you? Need coriander!

18.38 Made do with parsley, on your way?

19.05 Food under control but need help clearing up, sorting kids. Where are you!?

19.45 They'll be here soon. Tried calling. Where hell are you?

20.05 Are you OK Jamie? Worried. Please call.

23.35 Embarrassing! Said your mum ill and you'd gone to see her. What can I say? If it's Ben, you have every right to be angry, but only happened once, and didn't mean anything. Still love you.

07.30 Haven't slept. Kids will be up soon. What do I say?

08.43 Ben, I think Jamie has left me. Don't know where he is, won't answer his phone. Can we meet?

10.23 Ben, are you free? Kids gone to Mum's but only have couple of hours. Least you owe me.

11.15 Ben, Sarah just called. What made you tell her? What a mess!

11.37 Thanks for calling Ben. Understand you have responsibility to kids, course I do. And Sarah's lovely. Sure she'll forgive you.

11.40 Jamie, if you don't reply I'll call police. Typical of you to run away, like a coward. Dad always said you were spineless.

12.18 OK, things weren't great but let's try again, for kids' sake, please?

13.35 Jamie, Sarah's just called and told me all, about you and her. Bit of a shock but I suppose that's quits then? No reason not to come back and talk things over. We can work something out.

15.25 Please come back Jamie. Ben and Sarah are making a go of it, can't we? Make do and mend? Please?

The Third Man on the Moon

Charlie, my Charlie, died on his beloved Harley on the way back from Cornwall. He'd been to see the total solar eclipse – 'chance of a lifetime' he said it was. I had a call from the hospital but by the time I got there he'd gone. Only later I realised I'd heard about the crash, on the radio, that afternoon:

'And now time for a travel update. Ellie?'

'Thanks Ray. There are problems on the main A303 near Amesbury. This follows an earlier accident. So that means major delays for those of you heading back from the eclipse. Police are saying to expect it to last for several hours, until the accident is cleared way. No alternative route I'm afraid – just have to be patient and sit it out. Otherwise things are pretty quiet out there this evening Ray, all things considered.'

'Thanks Ellie. Have you entered our competition yet?'

'What competition's that Ray?'

'You have to name the third man to stand on the moon.'

'The third?'

'Yeh. Everyone knows about Neil Armstrong, and I think most people know the second.'

'Buzz Aldrin.'

'Exactly, so we're asking, who was the third? Any idea?'

'None whatsoever, I just read the travel news.'

'True, and a great job you do too. Thanks Ellie. So, once again, this evening's question, on our moon theme today, who was the third man to stand on the moon? I'll be giving the answer right after a bit of Talking Heads...'

So I looked it up. The third man on the moon was Pete Conrad. He died in July 1999, of injuries sustained in a motorcycle accident, aged sixty-nine, thirty years after he'd walked on the moon.

I still find it hard to make sense of it all.

I'm Glad a Crusty Stole Your Pizza

The effrontery was brazen, your consternation instantaneous. The horror that a fellow human had the audacity to swipe a pizza from under your nose, grab it from your very hand, then disappear into the crowd. We only had a glimpse but we knew his type – the dreadlock mane, tattooed chest, baggy shorts – a crusty.

'Probably gonna to feed it to his dog,' I said.

'Anarchist!' you growled. How more anarchic could you be than to steal someone's pizza just as it was poised before their watering mouth? That was the trouble with free festivals, they were free.

But I'm glad he did. Now, when I think of you on the UKIP stall at the village fete, I recall the epiphany of your first encounter with the forces of anarchy. This bright-eyed girl steeped in Palestinian sympathies, Poll Tax protest marches, Red Wedge, crying along to 'who's gonna drive you home?' The posters splayed across your bedsit wall, badges on your donkey jacket, a keffiyeh draped round your neck. United by injustice, we were champions of the oppressed. But then a crusty stole your pizza.

After that, the slow and steady road to the village fete. Disillusion with Militant, Kinnock, Oxfam (excessive overheads), a brief flirtation with the Greens, acquiring a wealthy husband, a hefty mortgage and a power bob, kids sent to private school, reluctantly of course.

But that day at the festival was the beginning of our end: I saw in your eyes an uncompromising fear that could never be assuaged. I joined VSO and you didn't. Who knows what traumas we would have endured together, or imposed on our children?

So, if the guy on the stall next to you proclaiming 'Britain First' looks familiar, stretch out a hand and thank him for stealing your pizza.

Sky Blue

A sky blue butterfly flits between bone-white slabs, each a memory of someone grasped from life, standing proud in military rows in this green corner of a lost world. My trusty stick shakes, frail tears shed in spasms for the fallen brothers I will never see again, here or anywhere. But also for the years of slow unseen decay; I am scarcely living, a survivor of the prolonged barren span suffered by a mere witness, while they are forever slaughtered, forever brave, forever young.

The butterfly lands on the stone where I stand – *Private Jack Lethbridge, Gloucestershire Regiment, 30th June 1941 age 19, For Your Tomorrow We Gave Our Today.* Each year my stoop brings me a fraction closer to the stark black letters.

The insect's wings itch to fly again and it continues its agitated apparently haphazard journey. My uniform, made for a bigger better man, barely keeps me warm in the bright morning sun, my medals no longer glisten. I feel invisible in my stillness, so lifeless a busy butterfly can land on my sleeve, fearless and naive.

Such a finely-crafted careless creature is no match for human will, even when exhaustion looms and my future wanes. If there is a plaintive bugler playing somewhere in the distance I can no longer hear him. Remembrance itself now lies beyond the living. For all I know I am utterly alone.

I clasp the butterfly in my skeletal hand and squeeze, determined to preserve its glory.

Our Little Jaunt

Have I really never told you the story of our little jaunt down to Villefranche, Marge and me? What a kerfuffle that was, I can tell you!

The hotel manager, surly chap, started to panic as soon as I told him. 'This is very bad, Monsieur, very awkward,' he said, sweating visibly. He could see his hotel's reputation disappearing before his eyes, so I thought what the hell, I'd better sort this out myself, take control. I could see he wasn't the sort to rely on in a crisis, spineless.

'Don't worry old chap,' I said 'I'll sort it.'

So I packed the car, I think I had the BMW at that time, or was it the Jag, can't quite remember. Anyway, managed to get everything in the boot, and was up and away before daybreak. Manager chap seemed a bit bemused to see me go but not too disappointed I must say. I didn't bother paying of course, it was the least he owed me. I reckoned with a bit of luck I could make the night ferry from St Malo.

Driving north I began to mull over what to do when I got back. My GP, Johnny Lawson - do you remember him? - well, he was an old friend of mine, decent chap, regular at the Club. I knew he'd sort this out. After all, I'd helped him out of a few scrapes over the years, like that messy night we had in Brussels with those German girls. Have I ever told you that one? No? Remind me to, it's a screamer. Anyway, the upshot was that Johnny owed me, big time.

By lunchtime I was making good progress so I stopped at a charming little bistro I knew on the banks of the Dordogne. Marge and I had stopped there once on the way down to the Med. Had good memories of the place so it seemed an opportune moment to call in again. I pulled off the main drag and was pleased to see it was still there. Not always the case, these little gems tend to come and go quickly you know, some bright young chef builds a good reputation and before you know it they're off to some fancy joint in the city. Anyway, by now the sun was high and it was getting hot in the car, so I made sure I parked in the shade. Turned out there was a new maitre d'hôtel but the food was still excellent. Had a first rate bouillabaisse followed by tarte tatin and a fine bottle of Chablis if I recall. In the circumstances I decided to give the coffee a miss, though I could have murdered a cognac, offered my compliments to the chef and headed off.

To be honest I'd spent longer over lunch than I intended and realised I had to speed up a bit. But the last thing I needed was to get stopped, nothing the gendarmerie like more than a speeding British motorist, What's more, they're known to stalk the main roads to the ferry ports; crafty buggers, bound to be a few hapless Brits running late. So I stuck to the limit as best I could. It was touch and go but I arrived just in time.

The ferry wasn't a problem, I had a couple of stiff drinks to calm the nerves. Didn't get a wink of sleep though. Thankfully I wasn't hauled over by customs for a random check on the way off which was a relief. That would have been a sticky one. As you know, it's only an hour's drive home from Portsmouth. Once I was in the garage with the door down I heaved a huge sigh of relief, I can tell you. All I had to do now was to unpack the boot and give Johnny a call.

I told him I needed a favour, explained the situation and reminded him about that debacle in Brussels. He said he'd call round after morning surgery. Arrived looking a little pale I thought, made a quick inspection and gave me the low down.

'Well, it's clearly nothing suspicious,' he said. 'A stroke, or a haemorrhage more likely. There shouldn't be a problem. You may have to explain why you left it a couple of days to report it though.'

'I've been away, in France,' I said. 'Just got back this morning and found her like this. There's a hotel manager down in Villefranche who'd be happy to verify it. I've already unpacked her stuff.'

Johnny nodded. 'I expect that will probably do it,' he said. Then he gave one of those heavy professional sighs, just to show he wasn't happy.

'It's what she would have wanted, Johnny,' I said. "Marge wouldn't have wanted me to have to go through the hassle of repatriation and all that stuff. And that poor hotel manager, I couldn't bear it. Let's face it, it's not like it's going to make any difference, in the long run, is it?'

Johnny could see my point of view.

'No, I suppose not,' he said, though he sounded a bit weary I must say.

And that was it, our little jaunt. Our last one as it happened.

This is what I think about now, what I might say, how I might say it, now I'm back at that very same riverside restaurant in the Dordogne, with Veronica, my second wife. I must say, I didn't think the food was as good this time, the beef bourguignon was a bit tough I thought, although you can't really expect things to be the same after all this time.

'Did you say you came here with Marge?' Veronica asks.

'Yes, once,' I say. I pause, wondering how to begin the story, how Veronica might react, what tone I should give it.

'Do you know what?' I say, 'I think the last time I was here must have been the day she died. I was on my way back from Villefranche. I've told you the story, haven't I?'

She holds my hand and looks at me sympathetically.

'You must have felt terrible, being so far away, not being with her… you know… when it happened.'

'Nothing I could have done apparently, an aneurism waiting to happen the doc said. Johnny Lawson it was, do you remember old Johnny? Anyway, it was a long time ago, Johnny's long gone. Liver packed up in the end, I think.'

She squeezes my hand.

'Tell you what,' I say, 'shall we have another bottle? Can't help thinking a fruity little Sauternes would go down well with the crème brûlée.'

She smiles at me and the story that had drifted through my head dissolves into so many other increasingly hazy memories.

I am not a Goldfish

Colin is planning a holiday to a distant island where it will be warm and sunny, and where he will visit ancient ruins, snorkel in azure seas, eat delicious seafood and drink chilled sparkling wines at a beachside restaurant. It will be memorable. He knows it will be because he's planning that it should be. Otherwise it will just be a transient experience, here today and gone tomorrow. And what would be the point of that?

Colin is planning to visit some temple ruins high up in the hills that date back to a time before Jesus Christ because he thinks that will be particularly memorable. He will take many photographs, mainly selfies, maybe shoot a video, and upload them onto his Facebook page for all to see, especially him. Hopefully there will be a beautiful sunset that will be just right to capture and share. Sunsets always get lots of likes.

Colin will buy postcards for older relatives and a few friends who are not on Facebook, so they don't miss out. He will also buy several tasteful souvenirs to add to his much-admired collection.

And in quiet moments when he's not recording his experiences for posterity, he will begin to plan his next expedition to acquire another batch of memories; maybe a jazz festival that he can film or a works trip to the seaside.

He does all this so that he can preserve his memories, lay them down carefully like a layer in the rocks, so that even when he only exists in other people's memories, his own will live on, like fossils.

I don't want to live in the moment, he thinks. After all, I am not a goldfish.

On Beauty

No sooner had we pulled into the car park at the top of the Alpine pass, than we piled out of the Renault to take in the panorama. It had been a hairy drive up the zig zag track, a series of hairpin bends taking us higher and higher, my father giving the impression of being confidently in command of the left-hand drive hire car, but my mother's tight grip on the grab handle , occasional strangled gasps and sideways looks of anxiety suggesting less confidence in our safety. We were glad to escape the tension, stretch our legs, take a look around.

'It's beautiful,' my mother said emphatically, gazing way down at a river of thick mist lying in the bottom of the valley, surrounded by steep slopes that swept up to a majestic range of snow-topped peaks. A flurry of cold wind flicked her blue and white striped skirt, her headscarf flapping excitedly. Finally, we were glad of our cream Aran jumpers bought especially for the holiday from M&S. My brother, a good foot taller but only two years older, already seemed to be outgrowing his. After a cursory look at the view and a quick cigarette, my father returned to the car to grapple with the Michelin map, trying to work out the easiest route back down to the comfort of the next Logis hotel and a bottle of cheap red wine.

'Don't you think it's beautiful?' my mother asked

us. We are a long way up, I thought, and the mist does make the view look… well, interesting, but beautiful? My brother concurred that it was definitely a spectacular view. I nodded, I could just about go along with that, it was a spectacle, but was it beautiful? It struck me then that I didn't really know what beauty was. What made a view, or a person for that matter, beautiful? Looking down from that Alpine car park, I could see something, many things, it was different to most views I had experienced, but I didn't feel anything.

The car hooted impatiently and my brother and I ran back to reclaim our seats in the back while my mother dallied for a few seconds, gazing out across the valley and the mountain peaks, arms folded, taking in deep breaths. Then she turned round and walked towards the waiting car and her three special boys, her skirt billowing in a lively gust of wind like a happy dog's tail, a broad smile across her face.

I think about this now as I sit by her hospital bed. She clutches a postcard in her fragile, lizardy fingers. It's a picture of the Rockies, from my brother, now living in Canada.

'It's beautiful,' she croaks and lays her head back on the pillow.

'It is,' I say, now I know.

Taken to the Brink – a Book Idea

I have an idea for a book. It's a reference book and it's called *'Taken to the Brink – 100 scientific ideas, discoveries and inventions that have led us to the edge of catastrophe.'*

Why? Well, personally I think it's high time we had an alternative history of science, one that recognises the role science and scientists have played, unwittingly, in the journey that has led us to the brink of catastrophe, to the destruction of the planet, and of mankind. No less.

From my point of view, bookshelves (and the media generally for that matter) are awash with glorifications of science, its heroes and wonders, its promises and solutions, its geniuses; there is little for a general audience that is critical of science, and that makes clear its central role in our predicament. In particular I think there is a lack of scientifically informative and educational literature that also points out the disastrous impact that many scientific discoveries have consequently had on our world. Instead there is an uncritical acceptance of the benefits of scientific progress. This book will highlight what I consider the elephant in the room – that the progress of science has taken us to the brink.

So, this book will describe 100 scientific ideas and inventions that have been significant in this journey to the edge of catastrophe. It will be presented in a straightforward reference format, nicely illustrated, and will comprise easy-to-understand descriptions of the science and technology along with the consequences for the environment and for mankind. In doing so it aims primarily to inform, to promote awareness of the underlying scientific and technological discoveries but also of their role in underpinning global warming, the denuding of resources, industrial pollution, the creation of weapons of mass destruction, cyberwars and other major threats to humanity.

I should make clear that this is not a book that presents scientists as evil geniuses or even science as a misguided enterprise. It is a history of clever ideas and well-intended people firmly embedded in their time and place. Nor is this an analytical expose or deconstruction of science, it doesn't try to explain why science has 'gone wrong' or present a critique of scientific method, but simply describes, in straightforward terms suitable for a general audience, the scientific discoveries that are pertinent to our predicament and why they are pertinent. For example, how the internal combustion engine works and how it has contributed to global warming, what nuclear fission is and how it led to atomic and nuclear bombs.

In doing so, I would like to think the reader is encouraged to reflect on the role of science, to question the notion of scientific and technological progress. But the book itself contains no polemic, just historical and scientific descriptions. This is not a manifesto. The intent is simply to make explicit the underplayed links between scientific discovery and environmental damage and all the other threats to our existence as a species.

I already have a chapter structure in mind, which will give you some idea of its scope. Each chapter focusses on one of the main threats to humanity and will include around ten of the key scientific discoveries that have brought it about.

1. Introduction – the antecedents of scientific discovery (fire, axe, wheel etc)
2. Global warming and climate change
3. Weapons of mass destruction (nuclear, biological and chemical)
4. Toxic pollution
5. The wholesale consumption of resources
6. Nuclear, chemical and biological accidents
7. Population growth and human longevity
8. Epidemics – diseases, viruses etc
9. Biotechnologies – genetic modification, cloning
10. Digital technologies – artificial intelligence, robotics, the internet, computer viruses
11. Scenarios for the future of mankind

The final chapter will present various feasible scenarios of the future based on our current precarious situation but in keeping with the nature of the book, will do so without making judgements or issuing calls for action. That's for the reader to consider.

This is a book idea that I hope someone else will have, someone who has the time, skills, knowledge and attitude to pull it together and persuade someone to publish. For me, it's an idea, but maybe for someone else it will be a project. If it is you, good luck, I'll be right behind you. All the way to the end.

Is There Anybody Not Waiting?

It was exactly as described on the poster in the surgery waiting room: aching muscles, painful joints, abdominal rash, stomach pains, feelings of nausea. See a doctor immediately.

I'm trying to.

That's me you see, those symptoms, no doubt. I know what to expect, a blood test and quick referral to hospital. Then, nothing. No one comes back, we know now. There are rumours, alleged sightings even, but nothing's been proven. There are stories, extraordinary stories, and theories, plenty of theories, some are plausible, but no proof, no hard evidence that anyone has ever come back.

Started about a year ago, reports of a mutant virus, deadly. Starts slowly, they say, nothing dramatic at first, feels like a heavy cold, bit of 'flu maybe, but gradually, inexorably, it eats away at your insides. Multiple organ failure, eventually. Can take days, weeks, months, but it is inevitable and there is nothing they can do about it. Except take you out of circulation.

E. mori they call it, short for something unpronounceable, Spanish I think. Supposedly started in Central America, caught from spider monkeys but God knows how. And who cares? It's here now in this city, in this waiting room packed with doomed faces. It's in me, and others probably, but nobody's talking.

I've heard vaccines are available if you know where to go, and can afford them, but I wasn't going to be duped. No harm in trying, they say, nothing to lose, what's the alternative? The alternative is to face up to it, I say. Have some pride.

And I remember the NHS. Not everyone believed in it but at least you knew where you stood. If there was a vaccine, you had it, for free, and usually it worked. Wasn't perfect but it was the best there was. Once the scientists came along, there wasn't much hope. Now there are plenty of vaccines, too many, too expensive for most and no evidence they work. Otherwise we'd know. Somehow, we'd know.

So here I wait, and wait, we all do. Occasionally a buzzer rings and a name is called out over the tannoy. Someone leaves the room. But for every one who leaves at least one more enters. Standing room only now. No one speaks, just a few sly glances, raised eyebrows, tuts and sighs, stoic stares. The frosted glass in the windows makes any view of the outside world impossible.

Then the waiting room door opens and a young nurse walks in, starched white dress and cap. 'Is there anybody not waiting?' she calls breezily.

She waits for a few seconds, gazes around the silent room, nods and walks out.

Then I realise. 'That's me,' I whisper, and follow her. But she's nowhere to be seen. I ask at reception. Nurse, what nurse? White uniform? We don't have nurses in white uniforms these days, dear. Why don't you take a seat, a doctor will see you soon.

But I'm not waiting. I'm really not waiting.

The Sensible Ending

Once upon a time, he wrote stories that went on for pages and pages, stories with intricately woven plots, carefully crafted characters, detailed descriptions of events and places, steeped in distinct colours, sounds and smells, characters eking out complex lives, journeys through time and space, other worlds experienced through the eyes of his fictional selves; a veritable filigree of language, dialogue, thoughts and actions, culminating in a subtle and profound denouement, a cleverly constructed, intriguingly ambiguous ending – the man left waiting for a taxi he knows will never arrive, a boy without a heart unsure if he will ever die, an author flummoxed by the behaviour of his heroine, a man trapped inside his own story.

But now he doesn't. Now he recognises the significance of a sensible ending.

Part 2

Shorts

The Taxi Driver's Husband

I sit in the hotel lobby, bags packed, waiting for the taxi I know will never come. It won't come because I'm not really there. And why would a taxi driver bother to collect a passenger who wasn't there? Of course, they wouldn't, but then this is no ordinary taxi driver, this is my wife. But then again my wife is not really a taxi driver, not a proper one anyway, she just pretends. She likes to go out in the evening, get out of the house for a bit, and I'm sure the extra cash helps, especially at the moment. Most of the punters don't realise she's not a proper taxi driver, and those that do probably don't mind because she's cheap.

I didn't know either, that she was a taxi driver that is, which is why it was a bit of a shock the first time she picked me up, especially as I was with Maria at the time, and we were both a bit drunk and very obviously together, if you know what I mean.

Which is why I'm here now, in this hotel room, bags not yet packed, taxi not yet called, alone without a penny to my name, nothing I can dispute with my wife through the divorce. All gone, mainly to this hotel in fact where I've been living for weeks, where I've been waiting for Maria, waiting for the taxi to bring her, driven of course by my wife. She would enjoy the irony, my wife, more than that, she would go out of her way to ensure the irony – it would appeal to her to drive her husband's lover to this hotel to resolve their future, all our futures. But it hasn't happened. Not yet.

I suppose discovering your wife has a secret occupation is less shocking than finding out your husband is having an affair (less shocking but more surprising perhaps) so we didn't get around to discussing it much. But I can understand the appeal – she is a good driver, enjoys meeting people and isn't averse to one-way conversations, I find.

Understandably perhaps her taxi business seemed to take off after that evening, and we didn't get around to talking about anything much for some time. She went out earlier and came back later, and who can blame her? By the time we did get to talk, there was nothing much to discuss.

'You'll be moving out I assume,' she stated abruptly one morning.

It could have been posed as a question but wasn't.

'Do you?' I queried mischievously.

She looked at me like I was an idiot, probably because she thought I was, maybe because I am.

She never asked 'why' which I was grateful for. It's a difficult enough question at the best of times and I wouldn't have been able to provide a satisfactory answer, for either of us. Maybe she already knew that. No, it was clear I had no choice, not on this occasion. She didn't even give me a lift to the hotel, didn't even offer me a price. She obviously doesn't need the money that much.

So I arrived here by tram.

'I'd like a room with a view of the taxi rank if possible?' I enquired, as enigmatically as I could.

The receptionist smiled kindly. She didn't ask 'why' either, which was good, and to be fair to her she did find me such a room. It wasn't a great view admittedly but I couldn't argue that she had ignored my request. She reminded me of Maria a bit, the receptionist, her smile especially, which is odd because Maria used to work in a hotel, as a chamber maid, before she was sacked for having sex with one of the guests. Best thing that happened to her though, as it happens – the sacking not the sex, I can't comment on the sex. The guy she'd been with felt bad so he got her a job in his estate agents, which paid better and had better prospects. I guess he had other ideas as well but she quickly dumped him, just after she got the job, just after she met me in fact.

'Don't trust her,' he said to me one time when I came to pick her up, 'she's only out for herself, for whatever she can get.'

I didn't respond, but what did he expect exactly?

She only lasted a few weeks at the estate agents before I helped her get a better job in the showroom of a local garage. Turned out she was a dab hand at car sales, had the right sort of personality, and looks, even though she can't drive. Gets loads of bonuses and hasn't looked back since, Maria. And I enjoy her gratitude, at least I did.

So who can you trust? The pretend taxi driver, the deceitful husband or his unreliable lover? Who can I trust? Sometimes I feel the burden of it all and I know I need something as grounded as a hotel bedroom – a private place that's mine and mine alone, a space that's mine but I have no responsibility for, a small manageable space that gets cleaned every day, with fresh towels and toiletries.

From where I can travel wherever I want through limitless television. And most of all, it's a room that locks, a secure room but also one that isn't so secure that I will think, stupidly, that it might last forever. That's not possible, obviously. It's safe for now but it's not a prison, or a home, definitely not a home. On good days, it's a base-camp for adventures, on bad it's at least a haven from the chaos, but that's my choice. I still have choice.

Where do I go from here? I could book myself back into the hotel – they don't know I'm broke, not yet. But Maria may never come, my wife may never bring her, and how else would she get here? Maybe my wife's taken Maria to a different hotel, the wrong hotel, either by design or mistake (she's not a proper taxi driver after all), somewhere they've never heard of me, and Maria thinks I've let her down, done a runner because it all got too much – it has been known. She won't be shocked or surprised.

Let me turn the television off while I'm thinking.

Maria is a wonderful girl, fiercely independent and energetic, but she's a lover not a wife and we both know that. I didn't even contemplate the idea of moving in with her. I knew she wouldn't want that and, to be frank, neither would I, even though it would have avoided penury. In fact I've not spoken to her since I've been here. She lives in a different world you see, a world where hotel rooms are for illicit pleasure, taxis sweep you quickly and silently to any destination, where, strangely, people really are what they seem, where lovers are honest and can be themselves even in their unreliability because that's what lovers are, what they have to be to be true lovers. It's a world I envy but cannot be part of now because Maria doesn't know where I am. She hasn't come.

'No, it's not the view, the view is fine.' The same receptionist and the same kindly smile, except maybe a slight hint of sarcasm this time, or was that just my imagination?

'No, there's this humming noise, at night. It keeps stopping and starting. It keeps me awake. Might be the water system or the air conditioner or something, I don't know, but it's keeping me awake.'

'OK, I'll see what I can do.'

'But I'd rather not change rooms. I'd rather it was just fixed if that's possible.'

'Of course, Sir, I understand. I'll get someone to go and have a look.'

Which she did, and it was sorted in a jiffy. Not a sound all night long. Every time I wake up, there is nothing, not a sound, perfect silence, just the occasional car passing by, on its way somewhere. Always passing by, never stopping.

Maria wouldn't know the taxi driver was my wife, you see, I never told her, that time she picked us up when we were drunk. She just dropped us at Maria's house as we requested and I thought it best not to say anything to Maria as it might have spoiled our evening. My wife fulfilled her role as a taxi driver without cracking once. Not only did she ask for the fare but I paid her, and gave her a tip! What was I thinking? She clocked where Maria lived of course, which was a concern, but then I decided that would be the least of my problems when I eventually got home. And it was.

But my wife would have known where to pick her up

now, Maria that is, when she called for a taxi – she even gave Maria her business card when she picked us up that time, which was a bit cheeky I thought but Maria took it as she liked the idea of a woman taxi driver. I imagine Maria would have recognised her, it being the same driver and, I don't know, but I suspect this time my wife would have introduced herself, knowing her as I do. Thus creating an interesting if rather tense situation – the spurned wife and the 'other' woman in the same taxi! What would they do? How would they react? Anything could happen! The possibilities are endless, too many to contemplate. Choices, choices…

'Well,' Maria might say to my wife, 'where do we go from here?'

'I'm the cabbie,' my wife would retort, 'where do you want to go?'

Maria would stare at her in the driver's mirror, and my wife would stare back at her. Not so much a stand-off as a sit-in.

But then my wife would break the ice – I know she would have the strength to do that.

'How about we have a trip around town, talk a few things over?'

And Maria would nod, probably not say anything but nod firmly and coolly to my wife reflected in the mirror.

Once they were in motion, conversation would begin to flow, a bit awkwardly at first I expect but then gradually more easily. In fact, they would be surprised how easy they found it to talk, once they got going. They would both find it easier to talk while driving or being driven, than they would face to face, in a bar or a café, or wherever.

The cabbie and passenger situation would be conducive to their conversation and they would unwind, slowly but surely, as the city passed them by on all sides. Things would be unwound, I'm sure of that, knowing them both, but the detail is a bit hazy at the moment.

They travel, and converse, while I wait here, neither in nor out. Wait until the chamber maid calls to clean the room ready for the next guests, and then I will have to go, allow the new guests to take over my space.

And I know, in my heart, it will be Maria and her new lover, the new guests. My wife and her latest fare, as it were, emerging from a strange meeting in a taxi, the gradual and clumsy uncovering of intimate knowledge of a mutual acquaintance and the creation of complex deceits and stratagems. It's not implausible, for either of them, take my word for it, I know them both well – an unforgiving wife and a lover who by nature is deceitful, both adventurous in their way, a combustible combination. They will take my room, my haven, and use it for all its worth, a passionate love nest for days and nights. More irony for my wife to relish, Maria and my wife together in this room, this very room, while I sit somewhere homeless and helpless.

Yes that's it. That's the way it is, the way it will be, has to be. It's not me they have any concerns about at all in fact, it's their own drives and desires that concern them both, that consume them both. My wife would come here to spite me, not to confront me, and my so-called lover would go along with it, for the ride, so to speak. That's their selfish self-gratifying way, and why I fell for them both at different times, in different worlds, and have now fallen myself, out of their lives. I'm superfluous it seems, or so it may seem to them anyway. Shows how wrong you can be.

Yet I'm pleased for them in a way – I like people to be happy – although it will be difficult for a while, difficult to come to terms with, for me anyway until I can find a way out. I'm sure it won't be for them, I don't doubt they will hit it off, in every sense.

'We'd like the room vacated by the man in the lobby,' my wife might say to the receptionist, 'the one sitting next to his bags, looking as though he's waiting for someone or something'.

'Yes, of course madam,' the ever-helpful receptionist would respond.

'And we'd like breakfast in our room,' Maria would add, 'and please don't have our room made up until we're ready.'

'Of course.'

The receptionist would smile knowingly, looking at Maria and thinking that she recognised her from somewhere.

I hope my wife enjoys Maria, as much as I have, we were good together, if ill-fated it seems. Maria has lovely breasts which my wife will be jealous of, but I'm sure she will admire them, she always admires other women's breasts. Even the lady in the lingerie shop remarked how lovely Maria's breasts were, but then she was in the business of selling expensive lingerie – a bit of flattery wouldn't go amiss, and it didn't.

So what would Maria see in her, my wife? Well, she is strong, confident – she knows her way around a bit, which Maria would find useful. She has contacts and she looks pretty good for her age too, and she has some lovely underwear. Then there are the free taxi rides of course. Maria doesn't drive but craves nothing if not the ability to move around at will, back and fro across the city, especially at night. She will enjoy unfettered travel, whenever she wants, wherever she wants, and my wife will be happy to oblige, at any time of day or night. I doubt she will charge her either, although you never know, she likes to keep her personal and professional life separate if she can.

But in the meantime I wait, bags unpacked, for the taxi I know will never come, driven by my wife who is no longer mine (or really a taxi driver), with her prospective lover in the back, who was once mine but is no longer, it seems, as they drive to displace and replace me, drive from my old house, where I never really felt at home, via Maria's house, which could never be my home, to a space I can no longer afford to keep but where they can truly be themselves. A chance to enjoy each other to spite me, create a new world they can share in this very room, probably in the lingerie that I bought both of them! It's beyond belief.

And so will I, start again that is. I have no choice but it is still a choice of sorts, I suppose. I have that at least, a choice, of sorts. What will I choose next?

It's time to go. Someone is knocking at the door. That usually means it's time to go. I expect it will be the maid, who is foreign and pretty and keen to make a new friend in a strange city, someone who will teach her English. At least, that's what she will say although really she's looking for an English lover who will teach her for free, and teach her the words she really needs to know and which will help her get on, which she will because she is clever and hard working and determined. I will teach her English because she deserves a break, she has earned one, and she is pretty which helps. Well, it helps me anyway and I'm sure she can use it to her advantage. If only she would stop knocking on the door, and shouting like that. She must learn to be patient. I will teach her patience, and buy her nice underwear, if she will just stop shouting for a bit, and stop impersonating my wife, or is it Maria, or maybe both of them, or the receptionist perhaps? Or even all four! Heavens knows, it's not an easy choice, it's not easy choosing. You ask too much of me sometimes, all of you.

I have chosen. I'll leave my bags unpacked, book myself back in to the hotel, go and see if I can secure a loan from the bank. I still own half a house, in theory, surely that will help? I will settle back in to my room, as I still like to think of it. That should stop the knocking and the shouting. I'll take a long hot soapy bath and let others chose for themselves how they want to live. That will be best. They must learn to live for themselves, make their own choices, somewhere else, without me. All of them.

I will lie naked in the bath tub and let the water rise up around me, slowly taking my weight. I will let the tub fill up as much as possible, and as hot as possible, making my face sweat and the steam mask my view of the bathroom, of everything. I will lie there in silence, careful not to spill a drop of water over the side, and wait.

Gradually, the water will cool and the steam will disappear. But I won't move, because it's so much easier not to. I will wait for the water to go cold, stone cold, until eventually I will concede and let the water out. But still I won't move, as the water seeps past my body and my weight returns – I will remain motionless until my cold naked body lies heavy and awkward in a hard, empty bath tub. Then, I may summon the will to lift myself out. I may. And if I do, it all starts again. Can I face that?

There's no point waiting for a taxi that will never come.

The Boy Who Was Born Without a Heart

How can you live without a heart?

The boy was around twelve or thirteen before he discovered he didn't have a heart, about the time I first got to know him. How he'd gone for all those years without anyone noticing, most of all himself, I can't explain, except that I suppose he was young and maybe just didn't know enough to know, as it were. But how come they didn't notice when he was born? Don't they usually check that sort of thing? Can't they tell straight away anyway? To be fair it was a long time ago, I doubt it would happen now.

All I know is that the boy was just coming to terms with his situation when his father died. I knew the boy well enough to be invited to the funeral but I hadn't really known his father. It happened not long after the boy had asked me to spend a weekend with him and his family and I had got to know him a bit, his father that is, but only a bit. He was a quiet, sheepish man who hardly said a word to me that weekend, but he wasn't unpleasant. He seemed to have a benign if largely mute presence in the family.

'Your dad doesn't say much,' I said to the boy.

'My mum makes up for him,' he replied.

The boy never cried about his father, who had some sort of heart problem himself it turned out. This hadn't been noticed before either, so maybe there was a connection, although he never suggested there might be. In fact he didn't talk about his father's death at all and I didn't want to pry.

I cried at the funeral and I didn't even know him, but the boy who was born without a heart just stood there by the graveside motionless and emotionless. At the wake, while his mother hustled and bustled and earned widespread respect for being a tremendous tower of strength, the boy appeared in a daze and was largely ignored, by everyone but me.

'He's holding it all in,' his mother whispered in my ear, 'it'll all come out later, mark my words.'

Maybe it did, I don't know.

Later that day, as I shook his hand to say goodbye the boy said, matter-of-factly, 'I don't have a heart you know.' I just nodded and smiled sympathetically. It didn't occur to me that he meant it literally.

'I really don't have a heart,' he repeated a few weeks later.

It was the first time I'd see him since the funeral. We were sitting in his bedroom, an unearthly hush hanging over the house, a sign of respect to the departed father – silence in memory of a silent man. His mother still hustled and bustled, but quietly.

'Listen,' he whispered and pulled up his T shirt.

It was true. However hard I tried I couldn't hear a thing, not a single beat inside his chest, and in a house where the sound of a pin dropping would have startled us.

'It can't be true,' I said.

'But there it is,' he said, 'or rather isn't. You get used to it after a while.'

It's difficult to know why he told me or why we became close as a result. I don't think it was really anything to do with his father's death but it did coincide. It gave him someone to be with who wasn't his mother maybe. I felt an attachment to his predicament, and maybe he was just relieved to reveal it to someone, a problem shared and all that. Whatever, he obviously felt I was the right person to confide his cardiac deficiency in. In doing so, he elicited a promise that I would never tell anyone. Even his mother didn't know, he said, or at least she didn't let on she knew.

'Don't tell another living soul or I will never forgive you,' he said.

So I didn't, not a soul. We became blood brothers of sorts, without spilling a drop of blood.

For years he never mentioned it again – why should he? – but it did eventually come up.

We were away for the weekend, in one of our regular bolt holes, and we were drunk (it being a bolt hole) but not especially so. He seemed a bit morose despite a good day's fishing and a hearty supper washed down with strong beer. He'd been married to Zelda a few years by then, had one small child and another on the way, a nice house and a decent job. He didn't say it in so many words but, despite all the signs of prosperity and contentment, maybe because of them, he was unhappy. For some reason he expressed this in terms of his own unique anatomy.

'This heart stuff gets me down,' he said, suddenly, out of the blue, 'why do I have to be so different? Why me? I didn't ask for this. It's not like it's my fault or anything.'

'What's the big deal?' I said. I had long since got used to his situation, and it didn't bother me, and he didn't normally mention it. He obviously got on perfectly well without a heart.

'It's easy to forget,' he said, 'I forget myself sometimes, but then I suddenly remember, it comes back to me. There's no escaping the truth. I don't have a heart.' I never knew him to cry but that was the nearest he came that day.

'I know,' I said, trying to play it down, 'but on a day-to-day basis it doesn't seem to matter that much.'

'It's not the day-to-day that's the issue. It's just that it's there, all the time, nagging away. Or rather it isn't, it's just not there, not there at all. There's just this black hole where it should be. All this day-to-day stuff is just a distraction, a way of avoiding the hole.'

He looked at me blankly, like you might look into a mirror.

'Fancy another beer?'

I think it was Zelda who came closest to discovering his secret. They were married for nearly ten years, had two kids, both girls, and all the trimmings. And then, one day, the boy got up and left. Of course, I knew things hadn't been going well but it was still a shock, to everyone.

Zelda was distraught at first, and then angry. During one of her many outbursts, she told me that she thought he was 'heartless', which made me wonder whether she knew.

'What do you mean, heartless?' I probed politely.

I found it hard to deal with Zelda, even though we had become good friends over the years. She had taken it badly and I don't think she saw me as neutral even though I tried to be. I was more a sounding board for her anger.

'What do you think I mean?' she fumed, 'he's a heartless bastard.'

Being familiar with his parentage I concluded she probably didn't mean either term literally, although I was never totally sure.

This made me wonder how close they had been. How well did she really know him? How could you be married for so long and not know that your husband doesn't have a heart? Had she never laid her head on his chest and noticed how quiet it was, like I had?

He still breathed of course, though how it all worked physiologically I was never too sure and I didn't like to ask. He may not have known, or wanted to know, himself but perhaps the rhythm of his breathing was enough to reassure her. Maybe she just never noticed that beneath the slow rise and fall of his rib cage there was no thudding pulse driving the blood through his body. Maybe she was content to assume that everything was OK inside, and why shouldn't she? What was there to suggest otherwise? Maybe he discouraged her from getting too close in case she discovered the truth. But then, if she had discovered it, what difference would it have made?

I never gave the game away and her anger never dissipated, from what I hear. We drifted apart, Zelda and I, gradually losing what we had in common I suppose. I don't think she ever knew the truth, although she got close to it. Close enough.

Life happens, as they say, and the boy without a heart lived and loved and aged. To me, he was always a boy, no matter how old he got. And he was always the boy without a heart.

He had colleagues, friends and occasional lovers but, as a far as I know, no one ever came close enough to him to discover that he had no heart. I had long since stopped being amazed that no one noticed. It is extraordinary but you really can live a normal sort of life without a heart. It just goes to show that we shouldn't make too many assumptions about what really matters, what is really required to have a life, and a reasonably good one as well many would say.

After the divorce he had, from my perspective, a pretty good time, shallow maybe in a way but you have to make up your own mind about these things. He enjoyed life, made sure his kids were OK financially, moved to a different city, bought a nice flat overlooking the park, all that sort of stuff. He put on weight, filled out a bit as they say, became paunchy others might say. He was in control of his life, worked as much or as little as he wanted to, played when he wanted to (hard sometimes), rested when he wanted to, more and more in fact. He ate and drank, often too much, when he chose to, was friendly and hospitable or morose and withdrawn as the mood took him. He depended on no one and no one depended on him. If ever I saw him, it was at my suggestion. He never seemed to mind seeing me, in fact he usually seemed to enjoy it, but he never called me, never took the initiative. He took life as it came, and he was content to let it come to him.

And don't forget, if you don't have a heart it does rather temper your approach to life. It makes a difference. You never know when it's going to all come crumbling down, so you might as well make the most of it, but then isn't that true for all of us?

But as he got older, his life contracted, and that's when the absence of a heart really kicked in, so to speak. Though she never forgave him, Zelda remarried and built a new life. As their own lives developed, his two girls had less and less to do with him. They weren't unpleasant towards him but they were influenced by their mother's enduring rage. And when grandchildren came along, it was easier to exclude the distant grandfather than the doting grandmother, not least because she was on hand to help out. In their eyes, he'd moved on, had a different life, one that he had chosen, although what that different life entailed they weren't really sure as they'd never been a part of it. It wasn't so much malicious exclusion as an indifference which they felt he shared towards them. What goes around comes around, heartlessness breeds heartlessness, I guess. He couldn't really complain, though he often did, to me anyway.

We kept in touch, being bloodless blood brothers, but weren't really close anymore. The fishing trips dwindled and the bolt holes dried up. Maybe he didn't need them, or me anymore, now he was his 'own man', with his own space and time. But the more he had, the less he wanted and his independence weighed heavily on him.

'My dream is to lie quietly on a tropical beach somewhere, without a care in the world,' he once said to me, 'and to really enjoy it.' I think that was the point – the dream wasn't just to be there, but to enjoy being there. That's what he found hard to do.

The boy had a long life despite not having a heart, maybe because of not having a heart.

'What you've never had, you don't miss,' he used to say

to me, when he was feeling positive, although I know he never meant it. After all, a hole's a hole.

There were some advantages. He was immune to some of those problems most people experience as they age – the clogged arteries, the palpitations, the aches and pains in your chest that make you sweat as you lay awake at night fretting. I doubt he gloried in it though, we tend not to celebrate the absence of pain, especially if you've never experienced that sort of stuff. And maybe he had his own aches and pains.

The last time I saw him was at another funeral. I can't even remember whose it was, there had been so many by then. There were only a few of us there, the survivors I suppose. He seemed especially quiet, even more distracted than usual. After the service, standing next to him in the chapel, I made some comment about his father's funeral all those years before but he just looked at me blankly. It was like he had no memory of it. I'm not even sure he knew who I was. 'I don't have a heart you know son,' he said dismissively, and shuffled away.

I didn't see him again after that. Why would I?

I guess if you're born without a heart there's nothing to stop you living forever.

But what sort of life is that?

Serious 'Cider

If I hadn't fallen from the bridge I would have been a branch manager one day, I know I would. I should have been a deputy branch manager as it was, even before the fall. But then it probably wouldn't have helped. Naomi, our legal eagle, might have given me a go but she could easily have found another excuse apart from my lowly status in the office, after all there were plenty of other reasons. And anyway I didn't want the job so I could pull Naomi, or to support Evie (my wife) in her selfless charity work, or pay for the twins to go to Disneyland (I'd always said that if I'd been on '*Who wants to be a Millionaire?*' and been asked how much I'd like to win, I would say 'enough to pay for the kids to go to Disneyland, and to pay someone to take them!'. I always thought that would have been a good line, but I never got on the programme, never applied to be fair).

No, the deputy branch manager job was mine because I felt it should be. It was what I deserved, simple as that. And I didn't get it of course – it went to Damien; this kid not long out of college, all short hair and smart suits and even smarter phone, works late during the week, on the slash at weekends, no responsibilities, turns up on a Monday morning bleary eyed but irritatingly smug. Probably enjoys our legal eagle's special rates as well. Naomi's known to prefer the younger ones though she must be well over forty. Can't blame her though – tidy for her age, kept herself in good shape by all accounts, and there are plenty of those, accounts that is. At least there were before Alison introduced this strict anti-sexism policy in the office. 'And that includes you lot as well,' she said pointedly to the girls, including Naomi. Now everyone's very quiet. Nothing much to say really, we all enjoyed a bit of harmless banter.

But he's a nice enough kid, Damien, I don't begrudge him and wish him well, but that's all he is, a kid. He has a lot to learn, about lots of things. I'd been up for promotion before, plenty of times, but this would be the last time, I'd already decided that. And it wasn't only about the job anyway, that was just the 'camel back breaker' to use one of Alison's favourite expressions.

When I was a kid, fucked-up 'ciders were always throwing themselves off this bridge. It was easier then, the parapet was only about four feet high, didn't take much to climb over. It happened so often that it didn't even make the local news. Some demented old tart's one hundredth birthday was more likely to feature in the paper. 'Ciders were treated more as a public nuisance. So much so they built a major structure, a sort of concrete canopy, over the road below the bridge so that the 'ciders didn't disrupt the traffic. But in the old days not much effort was put into stopping it. There was a sign on one side of the bridge that gave the Samaritans, telephone number along with the helpful news that the nearest phone box was 'on other side of bridge'. This was before mobiles and stuff so encouraging the poor sods at the end of their tether to call a sympathetic ear by walking across the bridge was tempting fate to say the least. A bridge too far you might say. If you were a serious 'cider you always aimed for the road. The result was guaranteed, whereas hitting the river offered the outside chance of survival, along with some nasty life-changing injuries most likely. So you stood a good chance of going from a bugger with some intolerable misery to being a permanently disabled bugger with the same intolerable misery and no means of getting to the bridge, much less jumping off it. Not the outcome you want, not if you were serious.

When the bridge was first built over the gorge, some Victorian tart jumped off and was saved from her doom by her dress billowing out in the wind as she fell, acting like some sort of parachute. They pulled her out of the river but they didn't record how grateful she was. Became something of a local celebrity apparently, used to wheel her out on special occasions like some sort of lucky charm, so maybe that cheered her up a bit. But survivors like her are rare and if you choose to jump off in clothing likely to cushion your fall in some way chances are you're not serious, more of a glory hunter. I have no time for attention-seeking glory hunters.

They said they'd built the canopy to save drivers from being hit by falling rocks from the side of the gorge, in which case why build it directly under the bridge and nowhere else along the side of the gorge? No it was really to avoid the nuisance of having bodies splattered inconveniently on one of the city's main arterial roads, to avoid having to close the road at rush hour and deal with disgruntled drivers trying to find alternative ways to get in and out of town. No more 'incidents' on the A4, no more overtime for police and paramedics needed to clear up the mess. Just a crumpled body to retrieve that could wait until a more convenient time. After all, it wasn't going anywhere.

By the time it came to my turn, they'd built a high wire fence along the side of the bridge. You had to be a determined 'cider, and a pretty agile one too. No good if you were some fatty who'd had enough bullying or a sicko wasted by drugs. You had to be strong enough and fit enough to climb up that fence and over the top. I managed it OK but it wasn't easy. Training's a good idea if you have the foresight – there are plenty of parks around with fences that are similar if you're interested and need the practice.

I like to think I fell rather than jumped. That's how I like to look at it. Anyone can choose to jump but I had no choice. It wasn't exactly an accident, of course I meant to do it, but it was inevitable once Evie left. Maybe I had been heading for a fall for some time but that was when it really kicked off, the beginning of the fall if you like. Not that I'm blaming Evie, not at all. I blame no one, except myself. I was a fall waiting to happen.

Evie left me, and took the kids, to join a travelling circus. Not a real travelling circus, obviously, but that's how I thought of them, Jim and his mob. After I kept failing to get promotion, Evie decided she was on to a loser and I guess the temptation was too much. Jim was the ringmaster, as I like to think of him, he pulled all the strings, kept the show on the road, and he had a whip of course. I found the whip under the bed one day. That's what triggered everything. Evie couldn't think of an excuse quickly enough and once I'd made her show me her behind, it was hard to deny something was going on. I never realised she was like that, but apparently she was. I'd have whipped her if she'd wanted me too, but it never crossed my mind she was into that sort of thing. I wouldn't have wanted to hurt her, deliberately but apparently that was because I wasn't a real man. Mind you, that was only one the many reasons she gave for why I was a complete asshole that she regretted marrying in the first place, many reasons, not all of which I can recall. Despising me for being the father of her children stands out though. I just remember that it was a long list which she'd obviously prepared for just such an occasion, a list that went through my mind as I fell but which escapes me now in detail. It wasn't nice.

I remember thinking that it would be just like me to miss the road, to miss my target – I was always missing targets at work. Sodding targets. I was doing OK, keeping my head above water, there or thereabouts, until the travelling circus came to town. Charisma, they were officially called, Jim's mob. What sort of name is that for an estate agent? Don't even call themselves estate agents, but that's what they are. They sell houses, over the internet. They're not much more than a fancy website really, not a proper outfit, not professionals. My lot, Shadbrook, Donner and Lowe (SDL as we're known these days) are well known in the region, been around these parts forever, branches in all the high streets, well established, but we couldn't compete with their pile them high and sell them cheap policy, Charisma today and cheers, thanks for your business, I'm off tomorrow. Quality didn't come into it, nor customer service, nor loyalty. They set up shop in the

Mall, in one of these pop ups, just to promote their website and get your email address so they can bombard you until you give in. Cheap rent, short-term commitments, recruited unemployed graduates from agencies and set about cleaning up on our patch, getting everyone to buy and sell on-line. Much cheaper of course, and people were daft enough to fall for it. Our long standing customers, the ones we'd nurtured, over generations sometimes, those who enjoyed the benefits of Shadbrook's personal, caring and reasonably priced (but not cheap) service. Here today gone tomorrow seems to be the order of the day. The travelling circus breezes into town with fanfares, cheesy radio ads and a social media blitz, promising the earth and delivering a cheap and anonymous service through some fancy software. It's not my world anymore, literally in fact. The meek shall inherit the earth? Not likely, the nerds maybe, graduates, twitterers definitely, circus folk. But at least I didn't miss my target this time.

Jim's really good with the twins, I hear. Of course, he is. He's got a trampoline too, of course he has. Got clowns and jugglers in the bathroom, bareback riders and trapeze artists in the garden. I expect Disneyland won't be far away now either, once she gets her money from our house and the spouse's death benefit from SDL (so glad I paid into that). I can see it now, they'll be off, spending like there's no tomorrow. I'm pleased for the twins though, hopefully they'll do OK, I was never able to give them much and Evie was right on one or two accounts in terms of my parenting prowess, or lack of it. Mind you, I suppose the attraction of Disneyland wanes when you've got your own travelling circus on hand.

I came up to the bridge by train from home. It's not that far, only a couple of stops but I didn't want to drive and then have the hassle of trying to find somewhere to park, and then having to buy a ticket, but how long for? The bridge is busy with trippers at weekends and on sunny days so I'd deliberately chosen a grey, wet Monday morning. I caught the train and bought a one way ticket. That's when it really hit me, the idea of a one way ticket, confirmation that you are not coming back. There's probably a song about it but I can't think of it off hand. Of course, there are lots of reasons why you might buy a single ticket, but in this case I knew it was significant. It made me sweat as I waited on the platform. This was it. So why don't I jump in front the train, I thought? Save time – not that I envisaged time being an issue for me. But then I thought that it probably wouldn't be going fast enough as it pulled into the station and it might not be that effective. Doesn't bear thinking about. If it was one that went straight through the station, as some do, then it made sense, but not if it was coming slowly to a halt. No, stick to the plan, I decided. I'd thought long and hard about it. I was serious, not a good idea to change your mind on a whim when you've made a serious decision.

Evie was a nurse when I'd first met her but she gave up work to look after the kids when they were little, which I didn't mind, but then she got herself an allotment, got involved in voluntary work at the hospice and created this busy life that meant she didn't fancy going to back to work when the kids went to school (not paid employment anyway), so I became the sole breadwinner, indefinitely. Not really what I'd envisaged you see. I thought we could share the work thing so I had time to develop other interests. It wasn't like being a branch manager was all I ever craved. There was more to me than that. Of course there was. But she couldn't see that. The drink didn't help I suppose. They say people drink to forget but I'd drink to try and remember who I really was.

At my interview, that last one, Alison asked me if I was a fruit, what sort of fruit would I be? I'd prepared all these answers to the sort of questions you usually get, like where do you see yourself in ten years' time? What skills do you think you can bring to the post? What would you do in your first hundred days? Those sorts of things. I had all the answers ready, the ones they were expecting, but I'd not considered what sort of fruit I'd be – I mean, why would you? – so I had to think quickly. I had no idea what they were expecting. There was a whole panel of them, four men, one or two I vaguely recognised from tedious head office awaydays, with Alison sat bang in the middle, staring at me over her half-moon glasses.

'A ripe banana,' I said, God knows why. There was a short pause.

'Why a ripe banana?' Alison asked, frowning.

Fuck knows, I thought, it was the first thing that came into my head.

'I like to think of myself as mature, ready for a new challenge,' I proffered, 'ripe for the picking,' I added, pleased with myself, momentarily.

'A bit slippery?' someone suggested.

'Soft on the inside?' added another.

'On the verge of going mouldy?' someone else chipped in, causing much amusement. I smiled vacantly.

'But why a banana?' Alison persisted.

Hadn't they had enough for fuck's sake?

'Well, I guess they are wholesome, nutritious, brightly coloured?' I offered in desperation.

'And a bit bent?' someone said, to guffaws all round.

This was out of order. It might not have been a sexist remark but it must infringe some equality law or other. I was tempted to say something but thought I'd better not.

'I hope this is useful to you,' I said, perhaps a bit too curtly.

'Yes,' said Alison with a steely gaze, 'it is.'

I thought it might be, though I wasn't quite sure in what way.

Later, I asked Damien what sort of fruit he's said he was. 'A satsuma of course,' he said, looking at me like I was some sort of idiot.

I hear Charisma are planning to move on, as a travelling circus would. Jim, Evie and the kids are going too, moving to Cardiff, moving school, house, everything, taking the trampoline with them. SDL will try and pick up the pieces, try and bring back a bit of custom, I'm sure Damien will give it his best, but it's not my battle anymore. I may not be a natural leader but I can see the writing on the wall. Alison looks to be in line for a job at head office but I can't see Damien being ready to take over yet. That's their problem, they'll have to look elsewhere. And rumour has it that Naomi is being headhunted by Charisma, personally, by the Ringmaster himself. Wouldn't surprise me. Good luck to them all. Good luck to everyone.

So fall I did, all the way down – it's difficult not to once you've started – and that was that. And this is this. Life gets faster as you get older, and ends in a rush. That was my experience anyway. Never underestimate the significance of a one way ticket, or a ripe banana. Keep that in mind. At least I was a serious 'cider. Still am. It's important to be serious about these things.

Jernees End

So to begin at an end, jernees end. Ere we is, back where we comes. Back on our knees at jernees end, down on our knees indeed. And luck.

Daymer told us bout life, how it spins, earth and moon, planets an all. Sum circly thing, he said, spose to go on and on, round and round, he said, summat like that. But no, not now anyways. Bin her before and it aint the same, no way. All dun and dusted, Daymer said, but no circly thing here, more a sprirally thing. Spiralling down, I says.

Only knows what was here before. Before Su, that is. Not what's in between, after begin and before end that is. I knows it there, somewhere, but god knows where. It's a mess, to be told, a true mess, so you can see for yerelf. Here is a begin and end, no midde just muddle, messes everywhere. That's down to Su, bloody Su. Tattered our tale, Su did, dam it.

Some say, it not the end that counts but the jernee. Jernees just a means to an end, I say, a mean means too. A mean means to a mean end.

So sorry, me mateys, youse has to make it up. Make what you will. Make it your will.

Here we is, me and Sham, peas in a pod you see, split eggs, spilled for sure, down at tide's long reach.

It's evening, another dam red sky. Day after day, sky after sky, nothing but red. Like the tree in the forest, me thinks, no dam noise when it crashes, not when it out of earshot anyways. Daymer told us that, wise bro.

Same on this beach, you see. No dam use this red sky, not now no one here to see it that is. None but us chickens, anyways. A muddle? Let me try, spite the spinning, all this spirally spinning.

Sham, my fellow egg that is, back to sea, no interest in the colour of things, no more anyways.

Daymer, Sham says, DAYMER!

No trees on the beach, like I told you, me thinks. Daymer done, me says, Daymer doing no more. Daymer ain't Daymer no more. That's the way of it.

Daymer, Sham says, DAYMER!

Still no trees on the beach, just dam red sky.

He was real sick, me says, Daymer was real sick, and then he was gone. Sick. Gone. That's the way of it.

S-S-Su, Sham says, so quiet to hear, me almost miss it. Speaks in shivers you see.

S-S-Su, he shivers, again. Me hears. He knows me hears. Bloody Su.

Su bin and gone, says me, bin and gone. Taken Daymer too, me says. Dam Su, dam to death. Bin and taken Daymer, ain't that a thing, eh Sham?

But he was sick anyways. I guess, sick and gone. That's the way of it, me shrugs, like you can shrug life away, shrug death away cos that all it is.

Sham, back to sea, don't shrug just shivers. He don't believe you can shrug stuff away that easy, not Daymer, not his bro, not our hero. He feels the weight of it all,

Sham, too heavy to shrug. I knows cos we're split eggs, you see, we knows our stuff, his and mine.

So here we is, at the end and begin, spiralling flotsam on a bloody shore. Me and Sham, two chickens in a pod, left for dead, left like the dead. Like Daymer, but not dead and gone, just left *like* we dead. On this bloody shore.

That's the way of it, I guess. Somewhere in between, water and sea that is, we wait and bleed, tween jernees start and jernees end. Left for dead in a spirally thing, like I say.

If I were youse, I'd leave us chickens down at tide's reach. Leave us stained by blood red sky, mourning in the evening. Take a look somewheres else, I would, look back up, right back up to jernees start. Good a place as any, I say.

Pass cross the seven seas and back – big black bastard seas – through the sunset to some dam old sunrise, less red though it's true. Daymer (yep, he again), fit as a fiddle now, playing the waves, riding, laughing, jiggling, now he sinks now he flies, fit as a fiddle-de-fucking dee. The world's his oyster bed.

Today, this day, the best day of my life, he thinks, the best day of my fucking life, he thinks. Daymer that is, though he ain't fucked no one yet, not yet. That's a tale to be told, to be sure.

Fifteen years and already happy, like a sandyboy. Am the happy sandyboy, he thinks, ain't none happier. Jiggling in a sea warmer than the warmest bath he'd ever known (he ain't known many). In love, the only love ever worth it, he'll think one day. In love with what's now, what's here, this warm sea and his bliss.

What to be done though? What to be done with being blissed? Don't think happy, just be happy. Best not to wonder why, he told us, wise Daymer. Easy to see now, of course, from down here, from down below.

Then Ma calls. Me and Sham, her little chicks, need sandycastles! Focus them Daymer, she says, while she stretches to the chalet for water. Dehydrated, she says, her favourite word those days, those warming days. Dehydration, source of all evil like water source of all life, she thinks. Keep them hats on boys, you hear. Keep them on, like hats the answer, the answer to every bloody thing. Keep them focussed while I'm gone, OK Daymer?

It's OK.

Then she's gone, stretching to the holy chalet, empty bottles of life clasped to squishy bosom. Not long, never long. Leaves Daymer in custody.

(No Da by the ways, never was a Da. Never missed him neither, not with Daymer as a bro.)

And he laps it up. Daymer growing fast, fit and fast, fit as a diddle. Not just a wave rider but now has two small custodies, two apprentices, two little beings to fuss. And build. Cos those were the days to build, build for the future. Build cos there *was* a future.

Build the sandycastles of our daydreams. Me and Sham real focussed now, hatted too, as if it mattered. Not just castles, fortifications no less, big words, Daymer claims them like a sage. Ramparts, turrets, motte-and-bailey, a moat dug down deep, deep as water deep in the sand. Daymer knows a thing or two to be sure.

Our little shared land of sand. Two growing grasping hands forge a tunnel through to Castle Yard, a road from across the desert from some distant land, Sandyland maybe. A tale, all told to listening twins, licking it all up we are...how our hero waxes as we dream of Sandycastle in Sandyland and all its doings, its comings and goings, it's like a little land so perfect, but so fragile to our clumsy. Easy to mess up, by accident. And we do of course. But that's all it is, clumsy, nothing more. Sandycastles so fragile.

Now I see, of course, just a matter of scale really.

Me and Sham, five years each back then (so fifteen ourselves now, maybees?), imagination without walls, focussed as our Ma's will promised, couple of learners clasped to our hero, carrying buckets from some piddle pool beyond the dune. To feed the moat, says Daymer, proud Daymer, a proper moat. Youse my helpers, he says, willing helpers too.

But water never behaves, now we know, sinks faster than we can fill. Daymer challenged, but he's up for it. Wait the tide, Daymer says. He knows it all, forces at work within his mighty grasp, we think, even when the water gone, O wise bro!

We know the tide anyways, we think – regulars on the beach, these sunny holy holly days. It goes, it comes, it fills, it flats everything, but always goes again. And comes again. We know the tide. Wipes clean twice a day, but you can always build again. Destroys, yes, but only for a while – playful destroyer. So far, anyways, we think, don't yet know the whole story.

Just a matter of scale really.

And before too long she's here now, Ma, back again, ample bottles filled with liquid life. Reliability her maiden name, our Ma. My little chickies, she says, thirsty little chickadees, dispensing bottles to thirsty workers. Quenched, they boast of their construction, and she admires, as she admires their everything, their every bloodless thing.

Ma Reliable, Daymer the King and his brother Princes, on the beach. What a wondrous land!

And so we wait the tide. Watered all round, shaded under our Ma's wing, needing for nothing, Ma and her three chickadees. Me and Sham focussed and together like something none can break. Bonded. And Daymer, in love and happy like he just been born again, or maybe born proper for the first time, this time for real.

Life begins, he thinks, watching the waves like some frolicking messiah. Down at tide's long reach. Happy as sandyboys, these diamond days. And no Da in the way of his manhood neither.

Life begins.

Those last lost diamond days, at some other jernees end. For not now, we know, not down here where the dam sun's bled all over us and Daymer bin and gone. Me and Sham, we sit, watered for sure, hatless and forsaken.

So tween these two seas there's a tale to be told, and there's the rub. A salty tale with a salty tail, as sure as eggs is eggs. We knows the begin in sunny frolics and blissed times, and we knows the despair of we twins alone, blood-tinged and forsaken. And between is a story of course. A story of Ma and her fortunes and frailties and fatalities, of Daymer's growing life, and loves, such loves, and heroics. Such heroics they made him sick. And Sham and me and our lives in and around each other, intertwined in Daymer's wake.

That's what this was, what it should be, you see – a tale of Daymer, Ma and her two eggs and their long jernee. A long tale, an epic jernee, a jiggling wave-riding jernee. Not this, not this stunted wastrel of a tale.

Cos here we is, already, at jernees end. Drowned chickens, dumped by Su, that bin and gone, and done this, we say. That dam moony thing, wiped away every thing, wiped out Daymer, though he were sick, but maybe not too sick. Wiped out Daymer and rubbed out our story, Su did. So all that's left is a begin and an end, and a mess. Such a clumsy mess. All over the place, words left high and dry, made senseless, stuff flung all over the shop. A muddled middle, nothing where it should be. Daymer gone and taken our tale with him, I guess. Left us senseless. That's the short not the long of it.

That's what it can do, you see, Su, what it can do to our lives story. Take a tale and make a fine mess of it, leave in tatters, just like that, just like this, here it was and then it's gone, from summat to nothing, like a fragile sandycastle in the tide. Clumsy S-S Su. No sense in it now, I says, no sense at all.

So sorry for that, me mateys, but maybees your tale better, more circly, with luck. Youse never knows, I say, and shrug. But Sham too heavy to shrug, too weighed down on his knees and all shivery, and red. Too far down maybe. But that's another jernee.

So make what you will. Make it your will.

Su Nami,eh? S-S-Su bloddy Nami.

Lobster Tails

I like to sit in bars and cafes and watch the world go by. But then, sometimes, the world stops and I find this disconcerting. I'd much rather it just went by but you can't make it. Sometimes you have no choice but to get caught up with it, and then things can get tricky. As I say, I'd much rather just watch it go by.

The world might come over and say 'how's it going, mind if I join you for a drink?', and then what do you do?

It happened only the other day, for example. I was sitting quietly outside one of my favourite bars, by the harbour, and the world appeared around the corner. Instead of going right by, the world stopped, put up a hand in recognition and said, 'Hi there, can I sit with you for a while? Be good to catch up.' I didn't feel the need to catch up but the world obviously thought otherwise. It's hard to say no.

'So, what is it with you and Cécile?' the world asks, sitting down opposite me at my small table. He looked a bit rough I thought, unshaven, dark shadows beneath his eyes, his voice hoarse; it had been a while since I last saw him.

'What's it got to do with you?' I thought, but it's better not to answer back to the world, I've always found, best to avoid riling the world, generally speaking.

'We're OK', I say.

'Come on,' he says.

The world, of course, has a pretty good idea about what's going on. You can't pull the wool over his eyes. Those sharp beady eyes, that large over-sensitive nose, those constantly flapping ears, he may not be at his best these days but doesn't miss much.

'OK, maybe things aren't so good at the moment.'

The world frowns and looks at me, as if to say, 'do you think I would have bothered stopping if it was just some sort of little local difficulty?'

'OK, it's not good. In fact it's really not good.'

'And?'

'And what?'

That look again. The world wears a black leather jacket over a clean crisp white T-shirt. Well, he would wouldn't he? Evidently he's too old for this hustler style, and he's not in great shape for his age it must be said, but he has the confidence, arrogance even, to pull it off.

'And then there's Véronique,' I say.

The world nods, a bit sanctimoniously I think.

'Véronique is a friend, a good friend, there's nothing wrong with that.'

'Nothing wrong,' the world agrees, but carries on looking at me intensely.

'So, what more is there to say?'

'Mind if I do?' he asks, picking up my bottle of wine in his enormous hand, gripping it all round and then twisting it as he pours, like he is wringing it into his glass, which had been my glass a second ago.

'Go ahead,' I say, perfunctorily.

'I don't know, you tell me,' he says and guzzles it down in one.

The world can be so patronising sometimes, but I try not to show my frustration.

'It's complicated, OK?'

The world nods sympathetically and pours himself another glass, this time truly wringing out the last drop.

'I know, it's never easy,' he says and slyly passes the glass to me, 'here, you need this more than me. Besides, it's a bit early for me.' Always that sense of superiority. I drink it, slowly, to show I'm not intimidated by his antics.

I hesitate to ask the world for his view, of anything. The world will have a view, I don't doubt, he usually does. But I'm not sure I want to hear it. So I don't say anything in the hope that he will go away.

But he doesn't. After an awkward silence while he sits there looking at me, I take out a cigarette. 'Mind if I smoke?'

'I'm not generally in favour these days, but go ahead if you must,' he says.

'You've changed your tune,' I think. I light up and blow smoke towards him, not aggressively but coolly, nonchalantly, as much as I'm able to be nonchalant in the presence of the world. He takes no notice of course. He's here, now and not going anywhere.

'It's a head, heart thing,' I say vaguely, 'you know what it's like.'

He looks at me like he has no idea what I'm talking about, but I know he does.

'I'm torn,' I say. That was the honest truth but even that didn't seem to satisfy the world.

'Look, I've got a lot to do,' he says, 'can we get a move on please?'

Get a move on? What was he talking about? I was quite happy watching the world go by, he didn't need to stop. But I keep schtum and finish my drink, slowly, sip by sip.

'I appreciate your predicament,' he says eventually, 'it really isn't easy.'

'No, it's not.'

'That's the way of it,' he says, shrugging his shoulders.

Why bother to stop by and interrupt my day if it's just to shrug your shoulders? How infuriating is that?

'Feel free to help me out,' I say, sarcastically, knowing that was the last thing he would do.

'Do they sell lobster tails here? I do love a lobster tail.'

'I've no idea,' I lied. I knew they didn't, of course they didn't, this was a bar not a café. What was he getting at?

'Pity,' he says wearily. But the lack of lobster tails seems to prompt a sudden thought, at last. He leans forward, pinning me with that penetrating stare.

'The way I look at it,' he says like there is only one way of looking at it, 'there are obligations.'

'Obligations,' I muse.

'Indeed. And then there are desires.'

'Clearly,' I think, 'the head heart thing, I've already said that.'

'It's an age-old problem,' he says.

How insightful, I think. He must be losing it. I've never known the world to be so pompous yet so tired, so downbeat. It was almost as if he himself felt obliged to disturb me though his heart really wasn't in it anymore.

He coughs and winces at the same time. I almost feel guilty for blowing smoke in his direction.

'You should think about it, carefully,' he croaks, thumping his chest.

I nod. That's what I was doing, I think, before you arrived. He leans back in his chair and wipes his mouth with a red handkerchief. He knows what I am thinking

'You can't always expect me to just walk by you know.'

My impatience finally gets the better of me and I brave a mild rebuke. 'Not expect, just hope maybe.'

He smiles and laughs, more a cackle really, flashing his yellow nicotine-stained teeth. I can smell his stale breath across the table. He's not the man he was but I still wouldn't want to get into a fight with him.

Just as I'm about to say something, the world stands up. 'Well, can't sit around here all day. Shame about the lobster tails.'

He looks at me like I'm a piece of shit, like it's all my fault, everything, picks up the wine glass and smashes it on the floor. And then walks away, away from the bar, along the jetty and out of sight. The last thing I notice are his jeans hanging loosely well below his hips, the top of his Hugo Boss boxers clearly visible.

The barmaid comes over but I don't think she'd noticed the world at my table, she just looks at me sternly. I smile apologetically, and start to pick up the pieces, the shards of glass that have spread all over the tiled terrace of the bar, trying hard not to cut my fingers, though I don't hold out much hope. The barmaid stands and watches, her arms folded severely, waiting expectantly for the first drop to spill.

That's the bloody world for you.

Say Hello to Ravi

The section on Mysore restaurants in my well-thumbed *Fodor's Guide to India* was encouraging; 'The food is first rate and inexpensive at Mister Dosa. Be sure to say hello to Ravi who has worked in this establishment for fifteen years.'

'This is Ravi,' the head waiter proclaimed almost before I had the chance to remove my backpack, 'he has worked here for fifteen years!'

Which was strange, because the bashful Ravi looked no more than twenty and my *Fodor's* was at least five years old.

But I could see Ravi worked hard to please Mister Dosa's patrons. His head constantly tilted and swayed in that unique Indian way as he attended enthusiastically to every customer seated at the long stainless steel tables. In fact Ravi appeared to be the only waiter in the restaurant, apart from the head himself who stood pompously by the door waiting to greet people and introduce them to Ravi, even while poor Ravi was frantically trying to cope with the many and varied demands of Mister Dosa's hungry customers.

'Just coming boss,' he said cheerily, juggling and delivering several thali trays to a table of dangerously gesticulating businessmen.

Clearly Ravi took his position seriously, and a bit

of complicity was the least I could afford to reward him with. If my battered, out-of-date guidebook bought from a second-hand shop on the Tottenham Court Road said there was a Ravi working here for fifteen years who you should say hello to, then so be it, that was fine by me. How could Mister Dosa disappoint foreign visitors travelling half way across the globe on the promise of an encounter with the famous Ravi?

Having budgeted for a gap year trip on the basis of my *Fodor's* out-of-date prices, I had got used to drawing out my meal times in 'inexpensive' establishments like Mister Dosa for as long as possible despite the frenetic chattering and rapid comings and goings of the locals. They regarded me as something of a curiosity, smiled at me unselfconsciously and often spoke to me in friendly and courteous tones about cousins of theirs who lived in London who I might know. To them I was neither one of the dying breed of hippy travellers for whom they had little respect or comprehension, nor one of the new breed of wealthy tourists who they despised for confining their experience of the exotic to the safety of a gated five star hotel on the coast. A brief but polite conversation and a parting reference to the beautiful Princess Diana or the great Ian Botham was usually enough to fulfil their fleeting interest in this lone English traveller.

So, engulfed by the pungent odours and myriad sounds of Mysore's Mister Dosa restaurant, I savoured slowly and deliberately a series of spongy idlis laced with powerful chutney and the inevitable masala dosa, accompanied by glasses of sweet refreshing chai, and my mind wandered to what may have happened to the original Ravi.

'This is Ravi,' the head waiter proclaimed, 'he has worked here for fifteen years!'

'Sixteen years now boss!'

The head waiter gave Ravi a long hard stare and took him aside.

'One moment if you please,' he beamed to the unwitting customer.

'It's fifteen, you silly fellow,' he whispered to Ravi, 'that's what it says in the book so that's how long it's been. No more of this sixteen years business nonsense.'

'But sixteen is more than fifteen, boss. Even better!'

'No it's not! What's better is what it says in the bloody book. You've been here fifteen years, that's what is says, not a year less not a year more. And if that's what it says, that's what it is.'

'Not if I go it isn't,' said Ravi defiantly.

Ravi was a proud man, even more so since he discovered that he'd been mentioned by name in a famous English guidebook. In the eyes of the head waiter, he'd also become difficult to handle, a bit above himself as far as he was concerned, but there were strict instructions from the proprietor of Mister Dosa to keep Ravi sweet, to make sure he stayed. He was good for business.

The head waiter put his hand on Ravi's shoulder.

'Look Ravi, when the book people come back, we will ask them please change it, OK?'

'But when will that be? It took them fifteen years to come here at all. It may be another fifteen before they come again!'

'I can't help that,' said the head waiter, beginning to lose his patience while maintaining his grin for the benefit of the increasingly uncomfortable customer, 'that's the best I can do. Until then, you've been here fifteen years, that's all there is to it. Don't forget who's the bloody boss around here. And don't forget who the bloody boss's bloody boss is either,' he added pointing up at the ceiling to indicate the direction of the proprietor's office.

As soon as the customer was seated and busy tucking in to some deep fried lentil vada, the head waiter took Ravi aside and tried to placate him.

'Look Ravi, my old friend, you've had a long and illustrious career at Mister Dosa, why throw it away? You're in the book! What does it matter if it's fifteen not sixteen? What difference does it make?'

'It's a lie,' said Ravi mournfully, 'it's not the truth,' he added to reinforce the point.

The head waiter had just about had enough.

'Go if you want, you silly fellow. Then you'll have to wait another fifteen years to be in a book.'

'So be it!' said Ravi and began to remove his waiter's jacket.

'Now you're being bloody stupid.'

But Ravi really had had enough. The truth mattered to him, and he was tired of Mister Dosa anyway, fame or no fame. He worked long hours and even on his occasional days off he had been told to be 'on call' in case a tourist turned up wanting to say hello to him. It was hard work being Ravi.

'Went to his head, silly bloody chap, had to go,' the head (and now only) waiter explained to the departing customers.

So Ravi left, confident that he could walk into another

job, a better job, on the back of a world-wide reputation, not realising until it was too late that his fame was completely bound up in being Ravi-who-has-been-at-Mister-Dosa-for-fifteen years.

'What benefit are you to me?' said the manager of the nearby Top Hole restaurant, 'what is the use of saying "this is Ravi, he is mentioned in an English guidebook because he was a waiter at Mister Dosa down the road for fifteen years but now he's working here"? What bloody use is that? You can wash up if you like, but that's all.'

Sucking hard on a beedi, the manager watched Ravi walk disconsolately out of the Top Hole restaurant, quietly pleased that at least Mister Dosa would no longer live up to its *Fodor's* entry, no longer have the advantage over his establishment of having a Ravi who had worked there for fifteen years.

Meanwhile, the head waiter at Mister Dosa had to deal with the predicament of life without Ravi. It was unthinkable not to be able to live up to the review in *Fodor's Guide to India*. *The* Guide, he reminded himself, *the* English people's Guide to the whole of bloody India, the entire steaming, teeming subcontinent. What would he say if a tourist wandered in and asked after Ravi only to discover he was no more? Not only would they lose trade, they would lose face, and that was far worse.

The proprietor, as the head waiter feared, made his feelings perfectly clear. He summoned the head waiter, by telephone, to his office on the second floor where he sat behind a desk piled high with pieces of paper, wiping sweat from his forehead, drawing on a fat cigar and sipping Johnny Walker. A huge belly strained his belt to breaking point so that he had to stretch to reach the papers on his desk, though he rarely bothered, preferring to lean back in his chair and gaze up at the ceiling fan rotating slowly above him.

'There will have to be another Ravi at Mister Dosa,' he said to the head waiter, slowly and pointedly in a deep husky voice, 'another Ravi who's been here fifteen years, simple as that.'

'But there isn't one,' said the head waiter plaintively.

The proprietor gave him a threatening, yellow-toothed smile and blew cigar smoke high into the air, 'then find one, you idiot. Or I'll find a head waiter who can. Now go.'

He dismissed the head waiter with a weary flick of the hand, dispersing cigar ash across the piles of paper in front of him, and took another swig of whisky.

The head waiter spent restless nights fretting.

'How can I find a Ravi who's worked in the restaurant for fifteen years when there isn't one, it's impossible!' he moaned.

'Advertise,' his wife suggested, sleepily, 'advertise for a Ravi who's worked there for fifteen years. You'll soon find one, believe me.'

He contemplated this suggestion carefully.

'Don't be such a bloody silly woman. How can you place such a stupid advert? Of course no one will apply.'

'Offer them a few more rupees than you normally pay. You see, I bet you'll find your Ravi.'

In desperation, he did advertise, and sure enough several candidates came forward, but they were all too young, and, when pressed, all admitted that Ravi was not their real name.

The head waiter despaired.

'Don't be so stupid,' his wife said the next night, 'look, it doesn't matter what their name is or how old they are. Think about it this way. Ravi-who-has-worked-here-for-fifteen-years is not a person, it's a job, a role you're paying someone to play. Who is going to quibble about their age and whether it's their real name or not? Hm? Tell me that?'

He thought about this carefully. It took a while to sink in. Ravi was no longer a person, but a job, a role. Of course, she was right!

'Don't be such a bloody silly woman,' he mumbled and fell soundly asleep.

As the head waiter's wife had predicted, for a few more rupees, a new, younger and more willing Ravi who, it seemed, had worked at Mister Dosa for fifteen years, was soon recruited. The new Ravi settled in well, quickly picked up the role and worked diligently under the eagle eye of the head waiter. It was hard work, especially with so little time off, but the new Ravi enjoyed the vicarious fame afforded by the Mysore section in *Fodor's Guide*. He showed the entry for Mister Dosa to his family and friends and explained joyfully, 'look that's me, I'm in the Guide!' They were impressed, if a little bewildered.

The proprietor, as he staggered through the restaurant on the way to his office, nodded to the head waiter, almost imperceptibly, which was as near to an acknowledgment that he had done something right as he was ever likely to get. The head waiter took comfort from his success as the proprietor's rasping lungs made their way slowly and painfully up the stairs towards the second floor landing ready for another hard day at the office.

All was well for a while, the reputation of Mister Dosa and the renowned accuracy of *Fodor's* famous guidebook restored. But rumours soon started to spread through Mysore's restaurants and tea houses that Mister Dosa was employing a young waiter to lie – there was no other word for it – to tourists about his name and how long he'd worked there. As far as its rivals were concerned, it was bad enough that Mister Dosa had been, unfairly in their view, recommended so highly in *Fodor's* in the first place, but now to exploit this in such an underhand way was beyond the pale. Something had to be done.

Matters came to a head and following a noisy and impromptu conference at the Station Hotel, the manager of the Top Hole restaurant agreed to take action, for the sake of all the restaurants and tea houses in Mysore city.

'Someone has to maintain the standards of integrity that our customers expect,' he proclaimed to unanimous approval and much back-slapping.

As agreed, the manager of the Top Hole restaurant approached the new Ravi on his way to work the next day.

'Ah Ravi, how is it going at Mister Dosa?'

The new Ravi looked at him blankly.

'It is Ravi, isn't it?'

'Er, yes sir,' he said a little hesitantly.

'The same Ravi who has worked at Mister Dosa for fifteen years?'

'Er, yes sir.' The new Ravi shuffled nervously.

'Of course you are,' said the manager of the Top Hole restaurant, airing his gold fillings. A smile spread across his gaunt face giving him a cunning, devilish look.

'You know Ravi, you can always come and work for me. The Top Hole restaurant is on the way up, you know. Business is booming and we need a new head waiter,' he said, carefully stressing the word 'head'. 'After all,' he added with a wink, 'with your many years' experience, you would be the ideal candidate. Good wages, no pressure to perform, every Sunday off. You can be your own man, so to speak. Think about it.'

The manager of the Top Hole restaurant grinned conspiratorially.

'Thank you sir, I will,' said Ravi.

'Good man,' he said, patting Ravi on the back, 'here, keep in touch.'

The manager of the Top Hole stuffed a packet of beedis in the breast pocket of Ravi's cheesecloth shirt and walked away, treading carelessly on the swathe of blood red stains splattered across the road side, left there in the traditional manner by the many passing betel nut chewers.

Ravi did think about it, and got back in touch with the manager of the Top Hole, and so another Ravi was lost.

'Who cares,' the head waiter's wife said, yawning, 'you can always find another Ravi–who's–worked–there–for fifteen-years. Believe me, it is not a problem.'

And she was right, again, and again. On a regular basis, in fact, as and when Ravi moved on to another position in response to a sudden need for a new head waiter in restaurants all around Mysore, there was always another Ravi waiting in the wings. After a while, Mister Dosa's rivals gave up trying to compete and learned to live with the reality of the situation as stipulated by *Fodor's Guide to India*.

'After all, it is in all our interests that tourists come to Mysore to visit this Ravi person,' conceded the manager of the Top Hole reluctantly to some of his fellow restaurant managers. It appeared that there were some truths that could not be disputed; greater powers were in force than they could counter, there was an order of things that had to be obeyed. But then, being Indian, they were used to that.

The good citizens of Mysore also got used to Ravi-who-has-worked-here-for-fifteen-years. In fact, the role of Ravi had become so well known that whoever it was became something of a celebrity in the city. Local customers, as well as tourists, would come to Mister Dosa and ask to say hello to the latest 'Ravi'. It became an in-joke; 'I know let's go and have a dosa, let's go and say hello to Ravi-who-has-worked-here-for-fifteen-years,' they would quip. And the head waiter and proprietor of Mister Dosa didn't mind one bit of course; it was good for business. Even the manager of the Top Hole wasn't too worried anymore. If Mister Dosa was full, as it frequently was, customers who had been turned away would often come to his nearby restaurant instead.

A battered road sign put up by the Mysore City Traffic Department had stood outside the Mister Dosa restaurant for years. It sought, unsuccessfully for the most part, to encourage drivers to slow down warning that it was 'better to be Mister Late than the Late Mister'. The proprietor added another sign next to it that said 'so drop in to Mister Dosa and say hello to Ravi who has worked here for fifteen years.' But the Mysore City Traffic Department got wind of this and had it removed, pointing out that it made it look as though the Department was promoting Mister Dosa, which it was not appropriate for it to do, 'although it had heard that it served particularly fine and inexpensive dosas'. Even the Chief of the Mysore City Traffic Department was a regular customer.

As the years passed, 'Ravi' became an increasingly privileged position in the city. People asked to have their photographs taken with him. He was invited to open garden fetes and new schools, and on one famous occasion, a particularly good looking Ravi was invited by the Mayor's wife to ride the temple elephant during the Dasara festival procession through the streets when garlands of rose-petals were thrown over the elephant and its rider as they passed on their way to Mahabaleshwara temple on the slopes of the Chamundi Hills. This was a highly prized honour to have bestowed on someone as lowly as a waiter. Admittedly, his selection caused a few eyebrows to be raised, not least by the Mayor himself, but it did nothing to stop the growing popularity of Mister Dosa, and of Ravi, even if that particular incumbent mysteriously disappeared one night without trace and the Mayor's wife was not seen in public for several months, only to reappear wearing silk scarves draped across her face at all times.

When tourists came to Mysore, whether for the Dasara festival or to visit the Maharajah's opulent palaces or simply to buy sandalwood carvings from the shops and street vendors around the main square, many would stop by Mister Dosa and enjoy their dinner served by the famous Ravi. Some got it and others didn't. Typically there would be conspiratorial smiles and winks as the invariably young (too young) Ravi waited on them, but some felt minded to write to the editor of the *Fodor's Guide* to point out the subterfuge. Yet, it was such a minor detail amid the intoxicating delights of the subcontinent that I doubt that few if any ever got round to doing so. And the good people of the *Fodor's Guide* clearly didn't feel the need to revisit Mister Dosa in a hurry, or if they did they were also content to maintain what must have seemed like a largely harmless myth.

Then, one day years later, late in the evening as the elderly head waiter was alone preparing to lock up, the original Ravi, down trodden and shame faced, and not a little intoxicated by arrack, walked into Mister Dosa to ask for his old job back.

'You must be bloody joking,' the head waiter boomed, brandishing his broom, 'you're too bloody old to be Ravi. Now go away and don't come back!'

Ravi shuffled away wondering how he had managed to become too old to be himself.

And that's how there came to be a Ravi-who-has-worked-here-for-fifteen-years at Mister Dosa when I passed through Mysore on my gap year trek through southern India. A wide-eyed, white-toothed young man, about my age, the latest incarnation in a long line of Ravis. By then there was not even any pretence that the chosen one was old enough to have worked at Mister Dosa for fifteen years, no less that Ravi was his real name. It had become another ritual in a land of rituals. Ravi, like so much in India, was truly ageless.

I imagine the original Ravi, the head waiter and his wife, and the proprietor certainly, have long since gone by now. But who knows, 'Ravi' may still be working at Mister Dosa in Mysore even to this day, aside the dusty streets infused with the fragrance of sandalwood.

And if he is, be sure to say hello.

The Leafcutter Ant

After the accident, and after her husband had left in search of work on the mainland never to be seen on the island again, the only job Maria could find was in one of the big hotels near the beach. It came with a room barely wide enough for the two single beds where she slept with her younger son Miguel who worked there too. When she wasn't working, Maria would lie on her bed watching soap operas, venturing out only occasionally as far as the Eroski supermarket to buy cheap gin, orange juice, crisps and cigarillos.

It was really only one job which she shared with Miguel, and only a single room, but Juan the hotel proprietor was an old friend of her father's and turned it into two jobs because he felt sorry for her. He remembered happier times when he was a fisherman and he and Maria's widowed father would play dominoes together in the evenings and drink Pernod in the bar where Maria's mother had once made the best paella in town before she became ill, and Maria played with dolls under the table listening to the dominoes clicking and the glasses tapping and the men cackling in the smoke-filled room above her. That was before the tourists arrived and Juan sold his fishing boat and bought the run-down old hotel on the beach and turned it into a veritable palace, while Maria's father's bar went into decline and he drank himself into the grave hidden from the world behind a scrawled sign nailed to the door that said 'please no food no tourists not at all thank you sorry'.

Maria's job was to replace all the chairs, tables and sun loungers left scattered carelessly across the hotel terrace. Every evening, when the sun had dipped in the sky and a cooling shadow covered the stone terrace, when the guests had returned to their rooms to prepare for dinner, and one of the waitresses had removed all the plastic glasses and other detritus, Maria emerged from her ground floor room to begin work. The terrace furniture had to be placed exactly, the dozen rectangular tables equally spaced in three rows along the side of the pool, each with four chairs, one at each end and two on the side facing the pool. The sun loungers had to be taken to the far side of the terrace away from the pool where Miguel would later stack them into neat piles. Maria wasn't able to do this because of the accident, which had left her paralysed below the waist and in a wheelchair.

To carry out her work, Maria had to go up and down the terrace in her wheelchair collecting and moving the furniture one piece at a time with an old snooker cue. Miguel had fixed a hook on the narrow end of the cue that attached to the feet of the chairs and sun loungers and the legs of the tables. In this way she was able to pull each item one at a time into the right position, scraping the furniture across the terrace, using one arm to operate her wheelchair and the other to hold the cue. It was slow but steady work which she carried out carefully and conscientiously.

Miguel often watched his mother from their room, thinking she looked a bit like a leafcutter ant transporting leaves to the colony, up and back, forwards and backwards, day after day. He would wait until she had finished moving all the sun loungers before going out to help. But he was also watching to make sure she didn't stray too close to the pool.

Of course he could have done the job himself in half the time, but he knew that she needed this job, to feel she had a job. So he would wait until she'd finished and had returned to their room and then go and stack the sun loungers, sweep the terrace and clean the pool. That was his part of the job, as well as doing odd tasks around the hotel when Juan needed some brawn, maybe a broken bed needed taking to the dump or some crates of beer or boxes of spirits needed to be carried from the van. In the off season, Miguel worked hard in the hotel gym to build his muscles which made him even more useful around the place. Miguel was a quiet boy but would do whatever Juan asked, which was appreciated, especially out of season when Maria's job took less time, and sometimes no time at all.

They'd been at the hotel for nearly two years when Miguel, who had begun to think of what else he might do with his life, asked Juan if he could help behind the bar. Although still young, Miguel thought this would be useful experience if he had the chance to have his own bar one day, like his grandfather. His mother spoke fondly and often of her childhood and he thought she might be cheered by the possibility that he might follow in the family tradition. Maybe one day he would marry a girl who could cook paella as good as his grandmother's and his mother wouldn't need to work at all.

Juan was happy for him to help in the bar, not least because he felt he was getting too old and stiff to cope with the many demands made on him as a genial host, not to say too grumpy to be genial in the first place – the sunny disposition crucial to his success as a hotel proprietor had been worn down over the years by, as he saw it, increasingly demanding guests. An English visitor had recently written a review for a website that said 'nice hotel, clean and tidy, reasonable food but watch out for the owner, a Spanish version of Basil Fawlty'.

Juan was astute enough to realise that this wouldn't do his hotel's reputation any good, so was keen to present guests with a younger, livelier and more amenable barman. Although Miguel had some way to go yet to overcome his shyness and gain the confidence and panache he would need to be a good host, Juan could see he had potential. He was honest, a hard worker and a quick learner, and had the natural advantage of being strikingly good looking. He was also cheap of course compared to employing an experienced bar manager, and with his mother limited in her capacity to gain work elsewhere, Juan thought that Miguel would be loyal , as well as reliable. After all, he was tied to his mother through tragedy, and his mother was tied to the hotel through necessity.

Miguel's only concern was that he would be on duty serving pre-dinner drinks when Maria started to tidy the terrace, although once the tourists were seated Miguel would be able to pop out and complete the job and still be back on duty in time to greet the well fed but seemingly unquenched guests as they emerged from the dining room. Miguel wasn't happy about leaving his mother alone on the terrace but was too embarrassed to explain his reasons to Juan, and he didn't want to pass up the opportunity he felt Juan had been generous in offering him. So he said nothing.

At night Maria lies awake looking up at the cracked ceiling, her head spinning from the heat and the gin and the agitation of ghosts. The ceiling is the surface of the water and she is lying below it, looking up at the wild rays of flickering lights, deafened by the turbulence that surrounds her, chaotic plumes shaking her head and bubbling up towards the light where she can see jets of water disappearing into the distance. Her son lies next to her in the water but while she scrambles around fighting for breath, he lies there still, floating serenely, his head hanging loose, his face obscured by a red mist that pours from his neck. Her arms flail about but her legs don't move. As he sinks slowly, she is dragged upwards by some unconscious force, leaving him behind, further and further behind, and as she rises the pain of separation sears through her torso.

She surfaces again into the arms of her other son Miguel who holds her tight, as he does most nights, gently shaking her from her nightmare. It's not his nightmare but one he knows all about for he has his own which he shares with no one. In his nightmare he is a young boy, not yet strong enough to swim across the bay, who can only watch from the shore, watch the speed boat bouncing across the water towards where his mother and brother are swimming. One day he will be strong enough to join them in their daily swim across the bay, but not today. Today, all he can do is watch as the boat strikes them. And then wade out towards his mother, grab her flailing arms and pull her from the water onto the beach. He comforts her, wipes away her salty tears and rocks her back to sleep. It is still dark outside their room, too soon to face the day. Sometimes he has to wipe away his own tears; he misses him too.

Miguel enjoyed his bar work. He had a natural charm and easy-going manner that the guests responded positively to, especially the younger female guests. Juan noticed that the hotel was proving more and more popular with groups of young English women with copious thirsts sporting matching, brightly coloured t-shirts with their names, or more likely nicknames, emblazoned on the back, wearing pink wigs and singing lewd songs into the early hours. Juan found himself increasingly intolerant of these groups but they had plenty of euros and Miguel would be a useful asset in encouraging them to part with them in his hotel.

After a few weeks Juan felt he could leave Miguel alone in charge of the bar and go and have an early evening nap. He would come back later when the revellers needed a bit of gruff encouragement to drink up and go to bed; Miguel was far too polite to them.

As soon as they had closed up, Miguel would return

to his room and find his mother snoring on her bed, the TV still on, often a cigarillo still smouldering in the ash tray and a bottle of gin on the bedside table, most likely half filled with tap water. He didn't mind so much if it was enough to take her through the night without the nightmares. If this happened they would be woken in the early morning by the rough sound of eager guests dragging the sun loungers back across the terrace to establish their territory by the pool before breakfast.

Miguel knew that it would be easier to stack the sun loungers nearer the pool but felt it was important that the tourists should have to make an effort. It shouldn't be too easy to bag a prime spot right by the pool; his mother should not be the only leafcutter ant around the place. She never asked why they had to be stacked so far from the pool. It was just the way it was.

Maria didn't mind that Miguel wasn't around when she started her daily chore of tidying the terrace; she was pleased that he was looking to develop his career options. Maybe one day he would have his own bar, like his grandfather (though hopefully be more willing to move with the times) and maybe she could cook paella there like her mother that would be the best in town. Adjustments would have to be made to the kitchen to accommodate her wheelchair, but that sort of thing was possible these days, she knew it was, she'd seen it on TV. Adjustments could be made.

Maria thought about this while she roamed up and down the terrace in her wheelchair, pulling chairs and tables and sun loungers back into their rightful positions with her trusty cue. Even the chairs closest to the pool could be retrieved from a distance without having to get too close to the edge.

One evening, towards the end of the peak season, something strange and alarming happened. A chair went missing. Maria had positioned all the chairs and tables and sun loungers that she could find but there was still a gap by one of the tables. She checked carefully again, the table only had three chairs and none of the others had more than four, there was definitely one missing. She wheeled herself around the terrace looking everywhere she could, behind the flower pots, behind the pillars that held up the wooden shading, among the sun loungers that were waiting for Miguel to stack, but without success. The terrace was enclosed by the hotel building on one side and by high, white-washed walls on the other sides and there was little chance that a chair could have been removed, not least because of the sign next the gate that led into the terrace that said quite emphatically 'please do not remove furniture from the terrace' in several languages.

As she moved around the terrace in search of the missing chair, Maria skirted the side of the pool and something caught her attention. She was afraid to look initially, but then she did and she saw that there was a chair, clearly a chair, lying on its side on the bottom of the pool, the deep end.

Maria was a proud woman, proud that she was able to hold down a job despite everything and determined that she should carry out her work as independently as possible. The easy solution would be to wait until Miguel came out from the bar to stack the sun loungers and let him sort out the chair at the bottom of the pool. But Maria felt she should be able to retrieve the chair herself, that was her job and it was quite likely that the cue would reach down to the bottom of the pool, it was not that deep. All she had to do was hook it through the base of the chair leg and surely she would be able to pull it out.

Surely, of course, but then again she was afraid to go too near the pool, and especially afraid to look into it. She knew why, Miguel knew why, he would understand her reluctance. He would not think badly of her and hopefully Juan would not notice the sunken chair before Miguel had a chance to collect it; she did not want to seem incapable of doing her job, she needed it. So she sat there by the pool, waiting for Miguel. But he didn't come that evening; the bar was busier than usual even during dinner.

At night Maria lies awake looking up at the cracked ceiling, her head spinning from the heat and the gin and the agitation of ghosts. There is no one next to her as she lies below the surface of the water, just an empty chair lying on its side. Where is her son? She needs to finds him, he was in that chair only a second ago! She tries to swim but her legs won't move and her arms are not strong enough to stop her from rising to the surface, leaving the empty chair abandoned on the bottom. The pain, the unbearable pain, sears through her torso.

Then she is by the pool looking into the water, looking down at the sunken chair, but it is not there. Instead there is a body there, the body of her son, his head hanging back loosely, a red mist pouring from his neck. She reaches out for him, she needs to be with him, to touch him. The surface of the water explodes but before she can reach out to him she is pulled away from the water, held and comforted by someone who looks like her lost son but isn't. They embrace and she knows her son is lost forever.

That night, beside the pool, Maria spoke his name for the first time since the accident:

'Ramon!' she screamed high into the night.

'I know,' said Miguel, holding her tightly, 'I know.'

'Ramon!' she screamed again, and some lights went on in one or two bedrooms overlooking the terrace, curtains pulled aside just a little.

'Sh, sh,' Miguel whispered into her ear, looking up at the windows and hoping none of guests would call out or come down to see what was going on.

'Let's get you back,' he said. She sobbed, tears dripping down her face. As he rocked her, her sobs slowly turned to shivers. Wet through from the pool, she was chilled by the wind that often came in off the sea in the evenings at that time of year.

Maria still wept as Miguel picked her up in his strong arms and placed her gently into her wheelchair.

'Let's go home,' he said.

In the morning Maria wakes, head throbbing, to the sound of sun loungers being scraped across the terrace. Her son, her only son, lies next to her in his bed asleep. He is still there and for that she is eternally grateful. He is a good boy, busy learning a new trade that will put him in good stead for the future when maybe he can have a bar and she can cook in a kitchen that's been adjusted for her needs. They work well together. In the meantime she has a steady job in a big hotel near the beach. It is useful work, and she enjoys the rhythm of her daily task – moving up and down the terrace replacing the furniture so that it's all ready for the guests. She and her son have a comfortable room and there is an Eroski supermarket just down the road which has everything she needs and which she can easily reach in the wheelchair by herself.

A Point in the Middle

The deep fast-flowing river that ran passed the house Jean had recently inherited from his mother was said to have its origin some fifty kilometres north west, high up in the Pyrenees, and emptied itself into the Mediterranean some fifty kilometres further south east after rushing through the quiet market town of Puivert on its way to Perpignan on the coast. This symmetry pleased Jean, he felt comfortable being in the middle of things. What's more, the ornamental metal cross erected as a memorial to his mother was, at her request, set on a small island right in the middle of the river directly facing the house. This was despite the protestations of Xavier, his neighbour, who reluctantly braved the strong currents in his rickety boat to help Jean fix the cross with cement in a sharp crevasse on the island.

'Stick it at the bottom of the garden,' Xavier had suggested, 'she'll never know.'

It was traditional in these parts that a memorial cross be planted in a chosen spot to favour the land bequeathed to a family member. So Jean, a dutiful son and only child, had insisted they row out with a heavy bucketful of rapidly hardening cement to the island to carry out her wishes.

'I'm not sure it even belongs to her,' Xavier had pointed out as he struggled to balance his boat alongside a precarious landing point on the rocky little island.

But to Jean, the stretch of river that flowed through his childhood was as much a part of his inheritance as the ancient farmhouse and the overgrown garden that surrounded and nourished it. He considered it entirely appropriate for her memorial cross to stand on an otherwise unnoticed island midway between source and sink, staking a claim his mother had willed and he was only too happy to respect.

Jean's inheritance was timely. He had recently separated from Yvette, his wife of fifteen years, who had been both the principal homemaker for them and their two children, and homeowner thanks to the generosity of her banker father. The spacious belle epoque apartment overlooking the sea on the fashionable side of Perpignan was a wedding present to them both according to the magnanimous speech made by the bride's father which was greeted with a hearty round of applause from the guests, but he'd not made his pile by taking risks with strangers and he ensured that, legally at least, it belonged only to his daughter. Something else for him to feel smug about now, Jean thought.

At Yvette's insistence, understandable in the chaotic aftermath of his careless adultery, Jean had moved out into a small rented apartment near his job at the university, where he taught philosophy. He considered it functional but soulless, a temporary but necessary solution until he found something more suitable. It had only been a brief fling with a fellow lecturer but he was not one for trying to manufacture an excuse for the inexcusable. Besides, he considered his infidelity a symptom rather than the cause, a symptom of something that had gone missing from their marriage, something that was in his view irrecoverable, perhaps inevitable. Yvette considered it a straightforward and unforgivable betrayal, of her and the children.

Jean's mother, ailing fast, was not made aware of the separation and the grandchildren were instructed not to mention it during their reluctant visits over the final few months of her illness as it 'would only makes things worse,' both parents told them. This didn't strike the children as any more odd than all the other odd things that were going on in their lives at the time, like having to sleep on spare mattresses on the floor of their Father's dingy apartment on the other side of the city every other weekend, and eat meals in a café with gruff Pernod drinkers who would pat their heads with rough hands and cackle menacingly while their father merely laughed and drank Pernod himself, seemingly oblivious to the evil intentions of his companions. And at least their grandmother's ignorance of the separation was something their parents agreed on.

The children's lives had changed and become distressingly unpredictable. Tempers flared, their equilibrium had been disturbed, which came as an unpleasant surprise. But such changes were inevitable, Jean told them, like losing the grandmother they had only recently come to know, and then only as an old and morbidly sick woman who lived in a cold, rundown house in the middle of nowhere next to an enticing river their mother warned them to keep well away from at all costs.

'Life's all about coming to terms with transience,' Jean said to them one evening in the café. His gruff friends nodded gravely.

'What's transcence?' the youngest, Michel, asked, yawning.

'It means it won't last,' his sister, Nicolette, told him.

'Oh good,' Michel said.

Once erected, even Xavier admitted the cross made an impressive addition to the view from the bottom of Jean's garden.

'There it is, fixed for good,' he said with a retrospective sense of accomplishment, 'always there for you. You can even see it from the top of the house I imagine?'

This was indeed the case. From the upstairs bedroom at the back of house that he had grown up in and was now his again, Jean could look down the garden to the river and see the cross glinting in the sunlight amidst the troubled currents. On either side of his garden, trees bent over the riverbanks, filtering the light and speckling the busy surface of the river, but right below the house the lawn bordered an open stretch that lit up on sunny days like an open air theatre.

After he moved into his mother's old house, Jean's children visited him less often. He was now a significant distance from Perpignan and although he was willing to pick them up, Yvette pointed out that the children had commitments at weekends like sports clubs and parties that they would miss out on if they were away in the country every other weekend and that this wasn't fair on them, what with everything else that had happened. She also reported that they had said they didn't like staying in the bleak rundown house anyway with its unhappy memories, nothing to do and no friends to play with. Nor did they like the food their father cooked. Jean wasn't sure whether this was really what they thought but when asked they seemed reluctant to either confirm or deny it and he didn't want to press them. Life was awkward enough for them as it was, especially when a new man appeared on the scene who apparently took them to swimming lessons on Sunday mornings.

'I don't want them playing in your garden without being able to swim,' Yvette told him, 'that river's a death trap. Claude's doing you a favour. I don't suppose you've got round to putting a fence up at the bottom of the garden yet?'

So that put paid to most weekend visits and Jean resigned himself to seeing his children only in the school holidays. He also promised himself he would try and make it more fun for them when they came and improve his culinary skills, which admittedly were not great. The two women he had lived with most of his life, his mother and his wife, had both been excellent and willing cooks and he never felt the need to challenge their supremacy in the kitchen.

Of course he had no intention of putting a fence up at the bottom of the garden. Not only would it spoil his view of the river, and of the island with the cross, but he considered these were as much a part of his territory as the garden and the house and wouldn't contemplate dividing any of it off. Even Xavier, though he questioned Jean's technical ownership of the island, was equally dismissive, recognising also that such an undertaking would inevitably involve a substantial amount of work on his part.

Xavier and Jean were not exactly friends – Xavier had not lived in the house next door when Jean was growing up – but they soon developed a pragmatic neighbourly relationship that suited them both. They borrowed from each other, and borrowed each other from time to time to help with chores neither of them could manage alone. Jean had much work to do on the old house that had become dilapidated over the years his mother had lived there alone after his father died and the extra pair of skilful hands, and tools, Xavier provided were often welcome. Likewise, Jean, less practical but younger and stronger than his neighbour, would often help out when a bit more brawn was needed. Few words passed between them beyond what was necessary to complete the task in hand, and with the exception of a small glass of Jean's best cognac to mark the successful erection of the cross on the island, they didn't socialise.

A few months after the memorial cross was blessed – Jean preferred to think of that as the landmark rather than his mother's death – Xavier asked Jean to help him move an old millstone that he wanted to take from the front of the house, where it sat next to the driveway, to the garden at the back of the house where he fancied it would make a suitably rustic ornament.

'It's a menace,' Xavier explained, 'I nearly hit it every time I come home in the dark. God knows what it's doing there.'

Jean thought this may be more to do with Xavier's wayward driving after an evening in the bar in Puivert than any intent by whoever had placed it at the front of house, quite likely before the driveway had even existed.

All Xavier needed Jean to do was to help him raise the millstone into a vertical position. After that, rolling it carefully along the side of the house into the garden and tipping it back to the horizontal was relatively straightforward. The task was accomplished with little fuss and bother though no mean effort was required to raise the millstone up from its initial resting place where it may have lain for centuries for all they knew.

'You're looking weaker these days,' Xavier remarked as he sat proudly on his new garden feature, smoking a cigarello. 'I don't think you're eating properly. I will send Cécile round with some food for you.'

Jean knew that Xavier had a daughter, his mother had mentioned her once or twice in passing, but he assumed she had moved away somewhere, to university or had got married perhaps – she was that sort of age. He had seen no sign of her since moving into the house and was now surprised to find that Xavier did not live alone.

'I didn't realise your daughter lived here,' he said.

'She leads a quiet life, of her own choosing. Doesn't go out much except to the market or to cycle to the cinema in town when there's some new American film to see. She's a good girl, Cécile, looks after me, her mother's daughter for sure. And she's a good cook.'

'That's very kind but I don't want to put her to any trouble,' Jean said.

'It's no trouble,' insisted Xavier, 'after all she owes your family. When my wife died and we moved here, it was your mother who taught Cécile how to cook. She was a wonderful cook, your mother, as you would know. It's only right that she repays the debt.'

'It really isn't necessary. I'm just a bit lazy when it comes to cooking for myself, that's all,' Jean said.

'It's no problem. She cooks every night. She can just make a bit more and bring yours round.'

Jean wasn't sure what to say. This felt like something more than mere neighbourliness and he didn't like the thought of being indebted to Xavier.

'And besides, you play the piano, right? I know you do, I hear you in the evenings sometimes, when the windows are open. Cécile will cook for you and in return you can teach her to play the piano. Deal?'

What had seemed a generous offer now seemed more of a premeditated proposal, but nevertheless it was one that did not seem unreasonable to Jean. They shook on it.

It was true that Jean played the piano but he considered himself little more than a competent musician. He had learnt as a child, taught by a great aunt who lived in Puivert and smelt of lavender and absinthe. He had played briefly and badly in a jazz band at university, but then let it slip once he had married and had children. He didn't even have a piano in the Perpignan apartment, although Yvette regularly said that they should get one so he could teach the children. It was only on returning to the old house that he felt moved to take it up once more, on the very piano he had first learned to play and which he swore still smelled of lavender and absinthe, though no one else appeared able to verify this.

'It's cassoulet. I hope that's OK?'

Cécile initially seemed a quiet, shy child whose most striking feature was her long auburn hair which ran all down her back, almost to the bottom of the apron she rarely seemed without. Jean thought of her as child and yet she must be about twenty. Her skin was pale and she tended to look downwards, even when speaking, giving her a submissive demeanour. But her eyes, when visible, also had a sparkle that suggested a lively spirit. She was not an entirely silent creature either, once she got to know Jean a little she became brazenly inquisitive about his life, his family and his work at the university. She said little about herself but learnt much about him, including that he had been granted a sabbatical from the university to write a book on 'subjectivity and the relative perception of time', something that took some explaining.

'Your children must love it that you write books,' she said.

'I'm not sure. They're still quite young, but maybe one day they will.'

Cécile was indeed a good cook – Jean's mother had taught her well – and she proved to be a receptive pupil too. On Sunday afternoons, she would come round for her lesson and he would teach her some simple pretty tunes that she could play to her father, on the piano in their front room which she revealed had not been played since her mother died, before they moved in next door.

'He misses her playing. That's really why he wants me to learn,' she said, 'but I don't mind, I like learning new things.'

It proved a good deal for them all – Jean eat well and enjoyed talking to Cécile about his life, Xavier was able to listen to the piano once more, transporting him back to happier times, and Cécile took satisfaction from cooking for someone as appreciative as Jean, and from learning to play the piano, and from pleasing both men in the process.

Until that was things changed again, something shifted,

and the river swelled with the spring rains, turning eddies into torrents that drenched the bottom of his garden and spat on his mother's cross. The Sunday afternoon tunes were interrupted, replaced by new sounds from Jean's room, where lessons in a different art commenced. Cécile was a willing pupil and Jean an attentive and sympathetic teacher. At first, sighs quietly and shyly uttered, then sharp gasps and lengthening moans slowly rising.

To Jean, these were sounds and feelings the house needed to give it new life, to blow away the dust and cobwebs of his mother's declining years; the sounds that marked the end of his mourning. For Cécile, this was the music she truly craved, the passions barely masked in the Hollywood films she watched in the local cinema with feelings of joy but also envy. These were the sounds of lives she thought she'd never live, but now she was.

One afternoon, as they lay on Jean's bed gazing towards the river, naked and sated with an ease unique to lovers, Cécile spoke softly about her mother, unprompted, as if something had been released from deep within her;

'She was so alive, so vibrant. She sang, she danced, played the piano. She always wore brightly coloured clothes; at least that's how I remember it. You wouldn't believe it but my father was such a jovial man in those days. He adored her. I think they were very happy.'

'It's good when people are happy together. It should be savoured.' Jean said.

'Why weren't you and your wife happy?' Cécile asked.

'It's difficult to explain. Our lives came together for a time, we were happy, but then we wanted to go in different directions. There were lots of fights and frustrations and resentments but really it was just that. Life pulls you apart sometimes. It's no one's fault.'

'That's sad.'

'Maybe.'

'For the children.'

'Certainly.'

'Do you think they will forgive you?'

For the first time, Jean felt irritated by Cecile's persistent questions.

'Forgive me for what?'

'For upsetting their lives.'

Jean looked at Cécile tenderly but recognised there was an unbridgeable gap between them. In many ways she was still a child, he thought.

'Instability is the norm,' he said, 'children in other parts of the world know that. I don't think we do our children any favours if we pretend things don't change.'

Cécile felt reproached and knew it would better to change the subject.

'My happiest memories are of my mother when I was a child, reading to me in bed,' Cécile said, 'especially the Greek myths. We didn't have many books so I'd ask her to read those over and over again. All the heroes and heroines, the good and the bad, the beautiful and the ugly, they seemed real but I knew they weren't. I suppose that's what myths are, stories that ring true, always, even though they were written so long ago about people and creatures that probably didn't even exist. I think children like myths, adults too perhaps?'

'Children are far more resilient than we give them credit for. It's adults that are less resilient, especially when they become parents, they become vulnerable then.'

Cécile twitched. 'Losing a parent is hard.'

Jean realised he had been clumsy but also sympathised. 'I know, even when they're old, it's still hard.'

She looked at him, straight in the eye for a change.

'You think I'm stupid, don't you?'

'No, of course not.'

Now it was his turn to look away. The bedroom was in need of a fresh coat of paint, he noted.

'I want to believe you,' she said, 'even if there is no reason to.'

The sounds of their lovemaking were the sounds of an intimacy that could not be shared but were also sounds that Xavier could not fail to catch one day, used as he was now to sitting in his garden on a Sunday afternoon listening to his daughter's weekly practice.

'Is Cécile unwell?' Jean asked when Xavier came round that evening with a bowl of thin chicken soup.

'Well enough to cook, but not to venture out,' Xavier said sullenly.

'I'm sorry to hear that,' Jean replied, sensing things were not right with Xavier, and suspecting he knew why.

'And she's decided the piano is not for her. She didn't want to tell you, didn't want to offend you, but I think it better if the lessons come to an end,' he said and turned to go.

'I understand,' Jean said. 'But it's a pity, she has ability.'

Xavier looked back at him with a hard stare that was both threatening and sorrowful.

'I daresay, but she is all I have.'

Jean nodded.

'Please thank her from me for all the wonderful meals

– my mother would be proud of her – but please also tell her it's about time I learnt to cook for myself.'

Xavier didn't reply. He had nothing further to say to Jean.

After that, Jean only occasionally caught sight of Cécile, when she was putting the washing out or gathering herbs from the garden perhaps, but she was too far away to speak to and although she sometimes caught his eye and smiled, it was the polite smile of a friendly neighbour not a lover's smile.

One day in the summer he saw her sitting on the millstone in the garden drinking coffee with a young man. Judging by the accomplished piano playing he heard later from the house, Jean concluded that Cécile had acquired a new, more appropriate teacher. He saw them in town soon after, on their way to the cinema most likely, cycling together, she in a yellow dress, seemingly carefree as the bike bobbed over the cobbled street. Her demeanour was different, more buoyant, her back straight and head proud as they sped over the bridge that spanned the river. She didn't appear to notice him sat in the café, where he went to drink coffee and make notes for his slowly emerging book, but just glided out of the village along the tow path, accelerating downhill in parallel with the tumbling river as it headed for the city and the sea, him leading the way with her following, her long red hair flowing behind.

On the anniversary of his mother's death, Jean sat in his garden, looking out across the river to the island and to his mother's cross as the sun set through the trees across the bottom of his neighbour's land. He had thought of inviting Xavier round for a drink, and maybe Cécile if it was allowed, but then thought better of it. He didn't want this to be an awkward occasion but a celebratory one.

So Jean drank a toast, alone, to his mother and to the river that flowed inexorably past his garden, from the hidden spring way up in the hills to its end somewhere downstream where it merged at some indiscernible moment with the unfathomable ocean. And, with his glass held high in the air, Jean thanked the river for passing through his world and giving him a glimpse of something that was neither at the beginning nor the end, but somewhere in between, a point in the middle, where it was, in his eyes, at its most majestic and vigorous.

As the sky darkened he threw the glass high into the air and heard it smash against the rocks that supported the metal cross, a memorial he supposed would last forever. A light came on in the house next door and a figure appeared in an upstairs window but he couldn't tell who it was and no sound emerged. Jean saluted drunkenly, whoever it was, as he meandered back up the garden. The light went out.

It was nearly the school holidays and his children would be arriving in a few days. He was glad he'd got back into playing the piano, and teaching. It was time they started lessons, Nicolette and Michel.

Jean would also teach himself to cook some of the recipes his mother had carefully written down in her best copper plate script in a set of hardbound notebooks that sat on a shelf above the range in the kitchen.

'They belong to the kitchen,' she once told him, towards the end, 'don't ever remove them. And if you sell the house one day, they should stay there, for whoever comes after. That's the way it should be.'

The Drive

He picked the girl up from her mother's house and they went for a drive. As he'd promised, they left the city behind, crossing the old suspension bridge that spanned a deep gorge cutting the suburbs from the countryside. As the rickety bridge passed beneath them, she closed her eyes and started counting, quietly to herself. She often went over the suspension bridge but would never look down, the drop frightened her. So she shut herself away from the world for a bit, until she knew she was safely on the other side. When the sound of the car changed and she knew the bridge was behind them she felt pleased, and today she was even more pleased than usual to be safely over the bridge. He sat there driving, oblivious to her silent ritual.

After the bridge, the road took them almost straight into narrow lanes and farmland. There had a been a light fall of snow that morning, not enough to disrupt the roads but enough to dust the fields and trees, to make them look pretty, she thought. The snow hadn't settled in the city so she was glad they'd driven over the bridge, even though she didn't like that bit of the journey. They'd not had proper snow for years, snow that made a difference, and she didn't want to miss it.

He drove carefully, edging slowly down a steep hill which she thought she recognised. The road was wet and slippery where the snow had turned to brown sludge and he cursed as a car passing the other way splattered it across the windscreen. As he cleaned the windows with the wipers, she wondered whether he regretted bringing her out here away from the city, but he didn't say anything, just concentrated on driving, on keeping her safe so she could look at the snow. After all, that was what they both wanted, what he said they could do when he asked her to go for a drive with him and her mother had allowed her to, reluctantly.

'Fancy some lunch?' he asked after a while.

She shrugged, happy to be driving around looking at the snow. She wondered how snowflakes, so small and fragile, could all but disappear into nothing when they landed on your hand and yet could stick together so tightly as to transform the landscape overnight, forming blankets covering whole fields, balancing themselves in neat piles on branches and walls, and when packed into balls could be hard enough to throw through the air and make your brother cry. She knew if she asked that he'd have an explanation but as far as she was concerned it was just fine that it did and she didn't need to know why snowflakes stuck together so well. She was happy to accept things as they were without needing any fancy talk on the laws of physics that she wouldn't understand anyway. Science was her least favourite lesson. She was content just to wonder.

'How about a drink then?'

She nodded and pursed her lips as if to say 'OK, if you like, but I don't really mind'.

They went to a pub in a small village where they used to go sometimes when she and her brother were little, he said. She didn't remember going there but she didn't mind. It was quiet and she felt grown up sitting inside with him, next to a log fire. She had a J2O and they talked a bit about school, about friends, those who were 'in' and those who were 'out', names he didn't recognise, about relatives he hadn't seen for a while, like her grandfather who she said was OK but he knew was dying, about her brother who was being a pain as usual, driving his mother up the wall. She was pleased to be with him but she got bored of talking and he ran out of things to ask. One J2O was enough and she still wasn't hungry. She liked listening to the fire cracking and the smell of wood smoke, and the murmur of adult voices, but he felt awkward sitting there in silence with an empty glass, knowing he shouldn't have another.

'Do you want to head back?' he asked.

She shrugged. She was rarely decisive, he noticed, usually happy to go along with what others wanted, enjoyed company but without wanting to lead. He knew this made her vulnerable but she wasn't one of the girls who was 'in' or 'out', she was always there or thereabouts. It wasn't a bad place to be, he thought.

'Or we could go for a bit more of a drive?'

She nodded.

'OK,' he said.

So they drove around the lanes some more, the lanes he knew from years ago, lanes that seemed to lead in circles sometimes. He drove so as not to stray too far from the bridge and the gorge, keeping near the fringes of the city, turning back when they got too close but not drifting too far away from familiar territory, or down lanes that seemed too narrow, that might be blocked by heavier snow or simply lead nowhere. This was a region of small hills, small villages, farmland and woods, a region he liked to explore when he was younger because it reminded him of his childhood, before he had moved to the city, before he was married.

They didn't speak much. She gazed at the snow blown across the fields and the woods and across the gardens of some of the big houses they passed. He had grown up in a house like that, with an overgrown garden and old trees, he told her. He had a tree house. He'd been lucky. At the bottom of his garden was a row of beech trees, like the ones they were driving past now.

She liked the beech trees; they stood in a neat line, equally spaced, whitened by snow but only on one side, sharpening their profile against the grey sky. They looked strange, a bit eerie, but nice she thought. She liked how the branches drooped, weighed down by their white load. She wondered how long it would be before the load was lifted and the branches could spring back up again. He drove slowly, more slowly than he needed to probably, watching her watching.

After a while they pulled into a layby and he switched the engine off. They sat there quietly and she thought he wanted to say something, and maybe he did, but he didn't. Now they were stationary she felt uncomfortable with the silence.

'It'll be gone by tomorrow, won't it?' she asked.

'I should think so,' he replied, 'there is no more forecast. And it's already beginning to melt.'

That's what she thought, that it would soon be gone,

but at least she'd seen it. She could tell her friends at school that she had been out into the country to look at the snow. She could tell her brother, who'd be annoyed that he hadn't been there, but she wouldn't say anything to her mother; it would only make her cross.

'Do you want to go and play in it for a bit? I don't mind.' She shook her head. It wouldn't feel right to play in snow just by herself, she thought, and besides, she didn't want to play in it, she just wanted to look at it.

As she gazed out of the car window, she noticed a young doe on the far side of the nearest field, picking its way gingerly along the edge of a copse.

'Look,' she whispered.

He followed her gaze.

'Do you think she's lost?' she asked.

'No,' he assured her, 'she's fine. She probably hasn't seen snow before. She's just trying it out.'

'You don't think she's lost, or alone?'

'No, she's just exploring. Her family won't be far away.'

The doe stopped still and looked towards them, and although it was some distance away it seemed to sense them. It suddenly took fright, jumped into the air and bounded away into the trees, creating a brief flurry of white powder.

'Why has she run away? Was she scared?'

'I don't think so. I expect she just decided it was time to go home.'

'She looked scared.'

'Maybe, for a moment, but only for a moment. Perhaps the snow scared her a little if she's not used to it. She'll be somewhere safe by now.'

'Maybe.'

'Come on, your mother will be expecting you back.'

The girl shrugged again. She seemed older already he thought. That was definitely a teenage shrug. It wouldn't be long before her shrugs would rebuff and beguile, her apparent indifference hard to read. She wouldn't be easy to get to know, but it would be worth it, he thought. She had a strong, quiet mind of her own.

'I know, let's go the long way home,' he said.

He started the motor and smiled at her. She smiled back; at that moment she wanted the drive to go on and on and never stop. She hoped, despite the forecast, there would be more snow, the more the better, enough to bury them.

But there wasn't. Not that day, or the next, or for a long time after.

Right there, right then, she was happy to be with him. They didn't speak much more as they drove slowly through the lanes, sometimes heading towards the city and sometimes away from it, but not too far away, not too far from her school and her friends, from her home where her mother waited, anxious and angry. The snow was melting fast, branches were dripping, more and more patches of ground were emerging and growing larger, and they both knew that soon there would be little left that was truly white and pure. It would all turn to brown sludge and then melt into nothing.

He knew this meandering, this wavering, couldn't go on forever. It was time to head back towards the bridge that would take them over the gorge, when she would close her eyes to avoid looking down, and count quietly to herself until it was safe to look. They would drive back into the city, and back to her house, that had once been his also.

It was a drive she would always remember, when she thought about him later, which she often did.

Voices on the Beach

Along the wooded path, he strides through dappled sunlight and sharp shadows, bare legs brushed by overgrowing undergrowth, damp stings flicking his calves, a prick on his arm from brambles briefly tugging at his shirt; these are the familiar marks of his pilgrimage. Accompanied by the chatting stones of unseen stonechats, plumes of midges sprouting from trickles of water, his pace quickens to the slowly emerging sound of waves and the unmistakeable smell of the sea. Senses primed, he turns the final corner into the stark heat of day, ready for what he knows will be there, waiting – the sounds, the voices, the fragrant memories that haunt his present.

This is how it is today and always was, he thinks. Then, when 'we were we', and now, still, when he is the sole witness, a lone traveller, the guardian of this seemingly deserted beach. Deserted but swarming with noises that greet him as the path turns to sand beneath his feet having accomplished its carriage, and the beach welcomes him with the warmth of an old and trusty servant. 'I'm back,' he says to the ghostly servant, who smiles and gestures gracefully to him to enter the expansive beach at his convenience.

No more than a chaotic babble initially, interspersed with the roar and crackle of waves, the flapping wind, the cawing gulls. But then as he sits down at the edge of the beach, back against a warm flat rock, taking in deep breaths of brackish air, the hubbub slowly distils into distinct voices that are his and his alone, inseparable from the beach they inhabit for as long as he is there to listen. Like the small rocks that pepper the shoreline, he has no choice but to allow himself to be immersed. It is, after all, the echo of his existence, a rhythm in his life as inevitable and unavoidable as the tide itself.

Just go in the sea, no one will notice.
Has anyone every told you, you look fantastic in a bikini?
Pass me a beer from the backpack Si.
You know, this would be a great beach if it wasn't for all these bloody kids.
I've finished my book, what else can I read?
Don't forget to send a postcard to your mum and dad.
Not here Deb, there are people watching.
So good to be away from work for a few weeks.
We should have brought some sandwiches, I just fancy a cheese and pickle sandwich.
Fancy rubbing some oil on my back Si?
I think you need to go in the sea to cool off a bit!
This is a lovely beach.
That woman over there looks just like Kate Bush, don't you think?…

I'm just taking Ellie over to the rocks for a wee, can you keep an eye on the stuff?
Don't be scared Ellie, it's only a dog, it won't bite you.
Look how happy she is, it's like one big sandpit to her.

Si, can you put the pup tent up, Ellie needs a sleep.
Where's Spot Goes on Holiday, that'll keep her happy.
I told you to bring the bucket and spade.
Quick Si, the camera!
Don't let her get sand in her mouth.
Why's that little boy staring at Ellie, the one with the big ears?
Don't let Ellie touch it, whatever it is.
For God's sake, why can't people keep their dogs under control?
I wonder if we'll see Kate Bush again this year?
No mobile signal here, that's good.
There seems to be less sand here than last year, don't you think?
What do rusks taste like?
What a lovely beach.
It is him, I'm sure it is, Damon Albarn, I swear…

Si, I'm just taking Finn over to the rocks for a wee. Can you keep an eye on Ellie?
Si, can you put the pup tent up, Finn needs a sleep.
Where's Spot Goes on Holiday, that'll keep him happy.
Daddy Daddy, look at my pretty shells!
Look Ellie, that boy with the big ears is here again.
No, you can't take that back with you, we've got enough pebbles at home.
Don't touch it Ellie, whatever it is.
Can we get a dog? Please, Daddy, please?
Quick Si, the camera!
Daddy, can you blow up my arm bands?
Why's Ellie got seaweed wrapped round her neck?

I told you to bring the fishing net.
Don't they look so sweet together, Ellie really likes Finn.
Don't go in the water without mummy or daddy there.
Right, I've got marmite, peanut butter or jam, what do you fancy?
Don't forget we need to send a postcard to granny and granddad.
Don't let Finn put sand in his mouth.
I'm sure there's less sand here this year.
Don't hit the ball so far Si, she's only little.
I don't know why I bothered to bring a book, I really don't.
Put some sun cream on Ellie, will you Si?
I recognise that woman over there, isn't she from Casualty?

I don't want a wee, I need a poo.
It wouldn't be a sandwich without sand in it.
Ellie, you can take your socks off, there aren't any crabs on this beach
Stop kicking the sand Finn!
He's just being friendly, Ellie, let him have a go with your spade.
Mind the green bits on the rocks, Finn, they're slippery.
Si, put some cream on your nose, it's looking very red.
Can you keep the dog under control Ellie, he's just destroyed that little boy's sandcastle.
Quick Si, the camera!
He's too young to hold a bat Si, he can hardly stand up yet.
Ellie's playing with the boy with the big ears again, they seem to get on well.
Daddy, can you blow up the lilo?
Look Finn's got a dead crab!

Isn't that the same book you were reading last year?
Right, I've got tuna, ham and tomato or cheese and pickle, what do you fancy?
Play together nicely, you two, no fighting.
I see a bit of the cliff face has fallen away since last year.
Come and put some sun cream on, you'll burn.
I told you to bring the body board.
Don't go in higher than your waist until we get there.
Mum, Finn's got sand in his mouth.
Don't forget we need to send a get well soon card to granddad.
Come and have a drink of water before you dehydrate.
Ellie, why did you give your spade to that boy? Now we'll never get it back.
Why is the sky blue?
Go and wash your feet in the stream before you put your shoes and socks on.
Isn't that Ryan Giggs over there playing Frisbee?...

You'll have to, there aren't any toilets here.
Come and put a towel round you, you're shivering.
Finn's buried my book and won't tell me where it is.
It wouldn't be a sandwich without sand in it.
Go and play further away, and take the dog with you.
Finn won't let me have a go on the body board.
My wet suit's too small.
Finn just kicked sand at me.
Don't climb up too high Finn, you might fall.
Last one in the sea's a sissy.
Come and put some sun cream on, you'll burn.
Looking a little podgier this year Si, those trunks a bit tight?

I can't believe there's no signal here.
Why don't you go and play further away you two?
Why is the sea blue?
Haven't we got a bigger spade, this one's rubbish.
Finn seems a bit wheezy Deb, do you think he's alright?
This is a lovely beach.
Stop fighting you two!
Si, what's that spot on your nose, looks like its bleeding?
Ellie, ask Big Ears if he fancies a game of cricket.
That bloody dog, bad boy Benji, put that spade down!
Quick Si, the camera!
Isn't that that woman from the X factor over there, whatshername…

You should have gone before we left the campsite.
Can you poke Ellie and see if she's still alive, she hasn't moved for hours
No Finn, hold the bat straight, like this.
I told you to bring the dingy.
Come and have a drink of water before you dehydrate.
His name's Jed, and his ears aren't that big.
Right, I've got cottage cheese, salami or cheese and pickle, what do you fancy?
Is that an appropriate book for Ellie to be reading at her age?
Don't swim too far out Finn.
Wet suits are for wimps, we never had then when I was a kid.
There's no point talking to her, she's got her earphones in.
I'm sure it will cheer granny up if you send her a postcard.
Why are clouds white?

Can we go abroad somewhere next year?
Those trunks are far too small for Finn, he's grown so much.
I don't need sun screen.
Why don't you two ever talk to each other these days, you used to get on so well?
It wouldn't be a sandwich without sand in it.
You're so embarrassing.
Ok guys, how many grains of sand am I holding?
How many years have we been coming here?
The guy over there with the beard , isn't he from Antiques Roadshow?...

Why do we have to come to a beach that doesn't have a toilet?
Right, I've got spicy humus, brie and grape or cheese and pickle, what do you fancy?
I didn't realise you can get a signal here now.
Finn, I've got your inhaler if you need it.
Having a bit of trouble getting into your costume Deb?
Si, cover up your nose, you know what the doctor said.
Come on Benji, keep up you poor old thing.
Ellie's bikini doesn't leave a lot to the imagination does it?
Keep the bat straight Finn and play through the line, like I showed you.
Stop looking at your emails if you don't want to know what's going on at work.
I see they've shored up the sea defences since last year.
Quick Si, the iPad!
Come and have a drink of water before you dehydrate.
Pass the Kindle Mum.

Keep your hat on Finn, you don't want sun stroke.
Why don't you invite Big Ears' Mum and Dad round to the tent for a drink tonight?
Perhaps we should ask granny to come with us next year.
It wouldn't be a sandwich without sand in it.
Whatever happened to the art of conversation?
For God's sake Dad, anybody who is anybody is not going to come here on holiday…

You'll just have to take a spade with you and dig a hole.
Hopefully the sun will be good for Finn's skin.
Don't swim out further than that rock.
I think I might get a sea canoe next year.
Don't forget we need to send an email and some photos to granny.
He's catching those waves really well now.
Haven't we got anything else to eat, I'm starving?
Your trunks really are looking a bit tight on you Si.
What's the point of sitting on the beach playing on your phones all day?
I've forgotten my inhaler.
Come and have some sun spray before you disappear.
Pass the Kindle Si.
Who wants a bagel, I've got salmon with cream cheese or cheese and pickle?
I'm going back to the campsite with Jed, it's so boring here.
Can I have that book after you, I forgot mine.
Don't go back in the sea yet Finn, you've only just had your lunch.
I was reading the other day that sun cream causes skin cancer.
Finn reminds me of your dad.

Do you remember the first time we came here?
You don't get the celebrities here like you used to…

At least try not to make it look so obvious that you're doing a wee in the sea.
It doesn't feel the same without old Benji.
You didn't have to hit the ball that far Finn, now you can go and get it.
I don't read books.
Have I ever told you I don't like cheese and pickle?
Si, put your hat on, you don't want to get another cancerous ulcer.
Any news from Ellie and Big Ears, are they enjoying Thailand?
I'm never going to grow old, or fat.
Finn, can you Facetime granny please.
Yes I know, 'it wouldn't be a sandwich without sand in it'.
Where's Finn, I can't see him, is that him right out there?
Do you think it's still OK to wear a bikini at my age?
Won't be long before the sea levels rise and all this gets swept away.
It doesn't feel the same without Ellie.
Pass me a beer Deb.
Finn doesn't seem interested in girls, or cricket, do you think he's alright?
Shall we get another dog?
You can't keep calling your future son-in-law 'Big Ears'.
I doubt Finn will come again next year.
This is a lovely beach.
I think there's a storm coming, I can feel it in the air…

When the voices subside he knows it's time to wander home, his audience with ghosts is over. But they will return, blown in on the sea breeze when he chooses to arrive, chooses to make the well-trodden journey to the beach. They will entice him here again, the green lanes and overgrown paths that line the way of his pilgrimage, for as long as the voices can endure the erosion of rocks and the rising sea. One day the voices will dissolve back into the cry of seagulls and thunder of waves, he thinks. Even memories lain down so carefully, so lovingly, layer after layer, can't survive once they go unrefreshed, unvisited, once they are disembodied completely. As it is, he is the only witness to those memories now, there is no one left to wave farewell to, except the trusty old servant, more decrepit with each visit, who bows wearily to the pilgrim as he takes his leave. They both know the old ways can't endure forever.

Walking back up the path he meets a young couple coming the other way, hand in hand, smiling. The man is tall, strongly built, wearing long shorts, carrying a bulging backpack, a man who looks as though he's prepared for any eventuality. She is small, red faced, her tummy swollen, walking awkwardly but with the confidence of someone who knows she can rely on the sturdy protection of her companion. The pilgrim stands aside to let them pass.

'Hi there! How far to the beach?' the man asks, cheerily, as he approaches.

'Not far', the pilgrim says, 'not far at all, just keep going to the end of the path. You can't miss it.'

He points, redundantly, down the path towards the sea.

'Thanks,' the man says, walking past him, beaming like an overgrown child himself. She smiles at him also but says nothing. The pilgrim walks on further but then turns and calls back to the couple, reassuringly.

'You can't miss it, it will be there, right in front of you, just keep going.'

'Thanks!' the man calls back and salutes. She doesn't turn but walks purposefully onwards, dragging him along like a pilot leading an ocean liner into a treacherous harbour. She seems to know exactly where she's going.

'All there in front of you,' he says to himself as the young couple disappear around a corner and some furtive creature scuttles through the nearby undergrowth. He turns away and heads inland as the blue hues of forget-me-knots begin to melt and a chorus of crickets herald the first murmurings of a whole new dusk.

'All there in front of you, one glorious, empty, silent beach.'

Life in the Chalet

Early in the morning, as light seeps into the chalet, the woman strokes her husband's penis. Only gently, she's not intending to arouse him. He's not asleep but his eyes are closed. He is still and silent but for an occasional murmur of acknowledgement. His penis doesn't grow. After all these years she knows what it takes. She knows what, when and how. And so does he.

The alarm goes off and the blinds clatter against the basin in the bathroom next door. A wind is getting up. Maybe it will blow in some clouds, she thinks, bring some cooler air. She's never known it as hot for so long, not since she lived down south when she was young, before all this.

The rhythmic breathing of the sea begins to lull her back towards sleep so she flings herself out of bed; she must be ready for work. Her uniform is a red T shirt with the name of the resort emblazoned across the front and back; 'Pacific Coast', in spidery white letters in the shape of a surf board. Her skirt is her own, black, short, the coolest she can find. Flip flops are OK, she's checked with the manager. She ties her hair back tight and is ready in no time. She'll grab something to eat and take a shower later.

A stone's throw later the woman is at Reception, looking

through the list of rooms that are ready. There's always a few empty by now, visitors heading for early flights or the morning ferry on the other side of the island at the start of long journeys home. Check out is midday but there is a steady stream of rooms ready to be cleaned or made up through the morning.

'Reckon it's gonna be another scorcher,' says the receptionist, smiling at her.

She's so pretty, the woman thinks, and so young. The girl is on a gap year before university, has a broad friendly smile ideal for the job. Jenni her name is, it's there on her badge on the lapel of her resort blazer. And there it is again, in the framed picture of the 'Employee of the Month' on the wall behind where she has pride of place shining between the resort's gloomy-looking founder and the puffy austere face of the current manager.

Is she Employee of the Month again or have they just not changed the picture since last month, the woman wonders? Guests are invited to vote so it's no surprise it goes to the smiley pretty one who greets them when they arrive and shares their excitement at the prospect of a sunny vacation by the sea. She's also the first point of call for any queries or problems, the face of reassurance and resolution. And then there's that beaming smile, destined to captivate. How can she not be the guests' favourite? It's not likely to be a maid, or a maintenance man let's say, those who work behind the scenes. Besides, the girl is staff not a volunteer, meaning she's paid not pitied. None of them have ever won Employee of the Month, which makes the woman wonder whether the volunteers count as employees at all. She doesn't even have a badge, but then she'd rather not.

'Any plans for later?' the woman asks, more out of politeness than interest.

'Oh, I'll probably join in with the surf school. They don't seem to mind me tagging along.'

I bet, the woman thinks.

'How's it going, the surfing?'

'Still learning, managed to stand up yesterday though, for about two seconds.'

'Awesome. Well, see you later!'

The woman likes Jenni, she's not immune to the friendly, breezy conversation, but she is keen to get to work, and to show that she is.

'Let me know when you're done,' Jenni says, 'I just have to tick things off, you know.'

'Sure. I know.'

The woman has plenty of experience as a hotel maid, it's what she did when she first came to these parts as a teenager, when she travelled up from the south looking for work, before she met him. It's steady work, not arduous or complicated. The woman finds it satisfying to clear up and make things good again, get things clean and straight, ready for returning visitors or new ones. She's not looking for awards.

And today there is a welcome bonus. In the first room she makes up, the woman finds a small kettle. A visitor has left a note next to it; 'not wanted on voyage, help yourself!' She puts the kettle in her bag along with another barely used bar of L'Occitane soap and some shampoos to add to the collection. There is already a kettle in their chalet but now she has one of her own; it might come in handy one day.

When he hears the chalet door slam, the man slowly gets out of bed, showers, gets dressed, grabs some bread and coffee, and walks across the beach towards the Point. He and some other volunteers are building a boardwalk so that visitors can take an evening stroll from the resort out through the forest to the lighthouse to watch the sunset without having to clamber up and down the rocks. The boardwalk will be subtly lit with solar-powered light studs so the visitors can wander to and from the resort safely in the dusk. They're planning to call it 'The Sunset Trail' which the man thinks is a bit over-the-top for a ten minute stroll but it's not for him to say. It's not a small job but the man likes to be busy, and useful. Besides, he has to earn his keep.

The man was a carpenter, before, and his job is to cut the planks for the boardwalk in the maintenance workshop which then get taken out to the path to be screwed into place on the runners, which he also made. This morning he's come out to see how it's going and estimate how many more planks he needs to cut. It's already mid-morning but no one else is there yet. Too hot maybe, he thinks, and maybe some are not as committed as he is. The plan is to have the boardwalk ready before winter sets in, so it's there waiting for next season, and they're way ahead of schedule. But there will be more jobs to do, he's sure, once this one is finished. The more the better.

As he measures the remaining distance with a tape, he hears footsteps coming along the boardwalk. It's not supposed to be in use yet, he thinks, haven't they read the sign? A fat American visitor appears through the trees, sees the path ending abruptly, well before his destination, shakes his head but smiles at the man.

'That's a really good job you're doing there, feller,' he wheezes.

'Thanks.'

'Did the other one get washed away?'

'No, this is new.'

'Huh, huh. Good idea though. Easy to twist your ankle on those rocks.'

'Sure, take it easy.'

The American gazes up towards the Point. He wipes his forehead with a cloth, sweat stains clearly visible on his shirt, spreading out from his armpits, a pair of expensive-looking binoculars hang limply round his neck.

'Is the lighthouse open?' he asks.

'No, it's never open these days. You can walk right up to it but it's closed, has been ever since…'

'That's a pity.'

The American seems flummoxed for a second, stares up at the clear sky. The man notes down some measurements on a small pad with a short stubby pencil.

'Is that a bald eagle up there?' The American points to the top of a nearby tree where an eagle is perched, looking out to sea.

'Sure is.'

'You have them here too.'

'Looks like it,' the man is about to say but then decides just to nod amiably instead.

'Oh well, I think I'll head back, no point in risking a twisted ankle. I have to drive back to the airport tomorrow. I know what my wife would say,' he chuckles.

'Have a safe trip.'

'Sure. Keep up the good work feller.'

He watches the American waddle back down the path and disappear into the trees, listens carefully to the clean sound of heavy footsteps on the planks until they slowly fade into the distance. Consider it a test run, he muses, sounds good and solid to me. He looks back up at the eagle, still staring out to sea like some unflinching watchman. Keep up the good work feller, he thinks.

After a few rooms, the woman takes a break. There is a wooden bench at the back of the main building, out of sight of the visitors' rooms, which has been designated unofficially as a volunteers' smoking area. She doesn't smoke but there's usually someone there to catch up with. Today it's Cindy, who used to run a First Nations craft gallery, but now helps out in the resort shop selling postcards, maps and beach gear. She has news.

'Hear Jim and Marty are moving out?' Cindy says.

'Where to?'

'They've got one of the new apartments up in town. They're prioritised because of Marty. And he's got a place at the new school too, starts September.'

'That's great. What's Jim gonna do?'

'Got some work fixing boats in the yard. Planning to save up and buy himself a new one. Get back on his feet, back fishing. He ain't gonna earn it here that's for sure.'

'Good luck to them.'

'Sure, but I'll miss them. I'll miss seeing Marty, he's a good kid. It's good to have kids around. Jim's been OK too.'

The woman knows that Cindy and Jim have become good friends. There are rumours but she doesn't listen. Cindy's fond of Marty too, maybe too fond.

'Not far to visit.'

'No, not too far,' Cindy draws deeply on her cigarette and blows the smoke high into the air, 'maybe I'll get one of those apartments one day.'

Maybe Jim will ask you to go with him, the woman thinks, but maybe not. It's complicated, she knows.

On his way back to the workshop the man takes the longer route to pick up rubbish from the beach. It's not one of his allotted tasks but he's happy to help out, and occasionally he finds things that are useful, like well-worn sculpted pieces of wood to decorate the visitors' rooms. The manager wasn't sure the bits of wood were a good idea but visitor feedback has been positive. The man has an eye for the right pieces. But today there is little apart from a few plastic bottles, a child's punctured ball, a few small bits of netting and feathered rope, too small to be useful. There's less stuff these days. It's a while now since he found anything he thought might be a genuine remnant, but he keeps looking.

Before heading for the workshop, he sits for a while on a log on the edge of the lawn overlooking the beach, takes out his pencil and notebook and calculates how many more planks he's likely to need and then adds a few more to be sure. The sun is at its scorching height and visitors have all but deserted the beach for the garden area where they can lie on loungers beneath the shady relief of fir trees and parasols. The tide is way out but will turn soon, he thinks, and then it will be a good time to surf.

At lunchtime they are back in the chalet. She puts out some plates of cold meat, fresh bread, a beer for him and some Coke for her. As she leans down to open the fridge door, searching for salad he comes up behind her, grasps her hips and rubs his groin against her butt. She closes the fridge door and stands so that he can clasp her breasts which are naked beneath her T shirt, kiss her neck, lift her skirt and pull down her pants. No words are spoken. She grips the fridge as she feels him enter her. She knows it won't take long, but that's OK she hasn't got long. Tonight it will be different.

After lunch the woman makes up the last few vacant rooms. Only one remains occupied. It has one of the resort signs hanging on the door handle; reads 'Happy Hanging In – Please Do Not Disturb'. She doesn't disturb but then just as she is tidying things away in the service cupboard a young couple emerge from the room heading for the beach. They are wearing swimming gear, carrying masks, flippers and towels – they look like resort towels, she thinks, haven't they read the notice? They are a handsome looking pair, she notes, tall, slim, athletic, suntanned, neat and tidy hair, hers long and blonde, his short and black, neat and tidy bodies too, unmarked. Honeymooners she supposes.

'Morning,' she calls down the corridor.

'Morning,' the young man says, slightly awkwardly. Is she being sarcastic saying morning when it was afternoon? He wasn't sure.

'OK if I make up your room?'

'Yes, of course,' he says, 'help yourself.'

'You might want to borrow a couple of these.' The woman hands them some beach towels in exchange for their bath towels which they hand over sheepishly.

'Thanks, we didn't…'

'That's OK. No problem.'

They seem a bit hesitant, a bit unsure of themselves, but the English often do, she thinks.

'Have a good day,' the woman says as they stride off. He gestures with a hesitant wave but his wife doesn't respond.

In the room, there are clothes and bedding strewn across the floor, a suitcase half unpacked, bits of leftover food on the table, an empty pizza box, a bottle of vodka, nearly empty, beside the bed. The bedsheet is stained in several places but the woman is used to that and pays no attention. Even the few drops of watery blood that have seeped through onto the under-sheet do not faze her. She opens the window to let in some air and watches the couple walk hand-in-hand across the lawn towards the beach. They talk intensely and move purposefully. They seem at ease with each other if not with the world yet. In her head she wishes them luck.

The man is not alone in the workshop. A couple of other volunteers are trying to fix a lawnmower while he saws wood. He has his own bench and tools. Not strictly his, they belong to the resort, but he's the only carpenter and everyone respects that. He grew up in this part of the island, started off as a lumberjack but moved over into carpentry, which he could do all year round. He likes to make things rather than chop things down, useful things like chairs and tables, things people need, and occasionally he carves wooden sculptures. Not found sculptures from the beach but ones he's made himself from scratch, usually as gifts for friends and family although he's not made anything like that for a long time now. He carved an enormous eagle for their wedding, painted it in the traditional way, erected it proudly in the garden. Lots of people complimented him on it. The neighbours used to bring their visitors round to see it. That's some bird, they'd say.

The man saws each plank slowly and precisely, to an exact length, and then planes them to a smooth finish. He strokes the wood like it was his wife's skin, until he's content. He knows they don't need to be perfect, in fact they don't need to be smooth at all for this job – once they're screwed into place on the boardwalk wire webbing is nailed on top to provide a good walking surface – but that's just the way he works, always has done.

'I reckon this is dead,' says one of the men with the lawnmower. He is the older of the two, called Scally though the man doesn't know if that's his first name, last name or just a nickname. He's never asked. Scally has lurid tattoos down both arms. He used to have a motorbike and knows a bit about engines so is generally put down for mechanical repairs.

'We should give it a go,' says Cal, the younger man with a deep red scar across his back like a whiplash, which it isn't. He goes round shirtless because the doctor told him to give it as much air as he could, even though the manager tells him to put his shirt on in front of visitors. Cal's keen to learn about engines, sees himself as some sort of apprentice, though Scally gives the impression that he's tolerating him more than teaching him anything.

'Don't suppose they can afford a new one at the moment, not until things pick up again,' Cal says, trying to sound knowledgeable.

'Give me a break,' says Scally, 'they're doing OK. We're free labour. Good labour too, skilled, look at the quality of those planks. And the government gives them a pile to keep us off the streets.'

'The chalets are free,' Cal says.

'Sure, but that's because they can't fill them. Not until things pick up.'

'They'll pick up soon,' the man interjects, 'then they'll want them back quick enough.'

'So what happens then?' asks Cal.

'They'll only keep the best of us, I reckon, the most useful, those who can make things, and fix stuff.' The man winks at Cal. Scally and Cal look at each other and Scally raises his eyebrows.

'Let's give it a go then Cal boy,' says Scally, 'that's what I always say, always give it your best shot.'

By mid-afternoon, the woman has finished making up the rooms and hands her key back to the receptionist. She likes Jenni for being as friendly to the volunteers as she is to the visitors – it's not the case with some of the others.

'Have a good evening,' Jenni beams.

The woman picks up a basket piled high with sheets.

'Just need to get this stuff to the laundry,' she says, 'then it's party party party!'

Jenni manages to keep her smile going until the woman's gone. She's not sure if the woman meant that or was being funny. Some of these volunteers are difficult to get, she thinks.

At the laundry, the woman catches herself staring into the machine as the washing tumbles around. It's a good day to be in the laundry with its windowless walls and stone floor, cool and shady, but the churning water makes her feel uneasy. She turns away just as a small boy appears in the doorway. For a moment he is unrecognisable; framed by bright sunlight from behind, his face is in shadow. The woman gasps but then the boy walks forward. It's Marty.

'Oh Marty,' she says, 'you gave me a fright!' Her hands shake and her heart thumps but she tries not to show it.

'Sorry.'

'That's OK sweetie. How's it going?'

'We're leaving.'

'So I hear. Exciting.'

He doesn't seem too excited. 'I like it here.'

'Sure. We like it here with you guys too. But it's good to move on. Your old man's getting back on his feet. That's a good thing.'

'I guess.'

'You know what, I bet once he's got himself a new boat he'll take you out fishing. Wouldn't that be awesome?'

Marty nods but he doesn't seem convinced.

'And we're not far away. We'll still be here. Us, and Cindy and all the others.'

Marty looks down at his bare feet. He understands what everyone is telling him. Hell Marty, she thinks, if only you knew. You're still here, take it. She smiles and gives him a hug.

'I know, how about you and me go and throw a frisbee around? This washing's got some way to go yet. How about it, eh?' Marty nods and runs out of the laundry. The woman sits for a moment, wipes away a tear with the back of her hand, takes a deep breath and then follows him out into the harsh sunlight.

The man has cut and planed enough planks for one day. No one has been in to collect them, take them out to the boardwalk, but that's OK, he likes seeing them lined up against the wall in a neat row. The lawnmower has been fixed, sort of, and Scally and Cal have taken it out onto the lawn to give it a go; he can hear it spluttering in the distance. Doesn't sound great but it keeps going. The man tidies away his tools, carefully and methodically, and then sweeps up the off-cuts and wood shavings and puts them in the bin. Only when everything is in its place does he lock up the workshop, ignoring the pile of tools and dirty rags left by Scally and Cal. That's their business.

After Marty is called for his tea, the woman takes the washing out of the machine and puts it in the spinner. She puts it on the timer to dry. It's supposed to go on the line, to save electricity, but she doesn't want to have to return later. This way she can pick it up on her way in to work in the morning.

She doesn't return to the chalet, knowing her husband won't be there yet, but walks instead across the lawn, passing Scally and Cal peering dispiritedly at a silent mower, and heads for the volunteers' area of the grounds behind the workshop. There she lies in a hammock in the shade of some fir trees, closes her eyes and listens to the quiet sound of waves breaking far off. It begins to feel a little cooler. Normally this is her favourite time of day.

The man is a consummate surfer; it's hard to grow up around here and not be. The waves are rarely huge but the bay is wide and flat and if you hit the right wave at the right time you can ride a long way. It's not a place for the hip surfing dudes, who hang out further south where there are big breakers and smoke-filled shacks all along the shore , but it's a good place to learn, to ride easy waves, and a good place to avoid the hip surfing dudes.

Today there is little wind and the waves are only a few feet high but the man still paddles out on his board as far as he can to catch a wave, relishing those moments of calm while he watches and waits for the right one, gazing back sometimes at the resort, partly hidden behind the line of fir trees that mark the edge of the gardens above the beach, bobbing gently in the clear water until the swell builds again and he readies the board to catch a wave just as it begins to break; he rarely chooses a dud one. And then the rush that comes from skimming across the flat surface, the illusion of speed as the water shoots towards and under him, twisting the board with his feet, sometimes to stay upright and sometimes just because he can, taming the power of the wave for pleasure, riding for as long as he can before his momentum finally falters and he falls from the board into the cool shallows. Quickly, he retrieves his board, so the cycle can start over again. One more, he says to himself, one more ride, he says time and time again.

He reckons he's surfed more days than not in his life, even in winter when there is ice on the rocks, snow drips from the trees, and the water stings his face. He can't imagine not being able to, it would be like there was something missing.

The woman wakes with a jolt, unsure how long she has dozed. She was dreaming, she thinks, but whatever it was has already gone. There is an airplane high above, set clear against the cloudless blue sky. There is no vapour trail which makes flying look so effortless, serene, harmless, she thinks. No indication of the noise, the emissions. This is our lifeblood now though, she knows, these plane loads of visitors, the best chance we've got to rebuild. Ironic! She doesn't like the idea of an influx of visitors but she knows how important it is, and how empty it felt when there were none, what their absence meant, on top of everything else. And she knows the government won't, can't keep on paying. They have to get back on their feet she knows that. Just enough visitors to help, she thinks, but not too many.

The chalet only has one main room, a bedroom come sitting room, with a small kitchen behind a screen in the corner and a bathroom to the side. They weren't designed to be lived in but it does for them. There is a view of the sea between trees and an outside patio area big enough for a table and a couple of chairs. They can sit out in the evenings if they want, though they rarely do. In winter, ice coats the inside of the windows and their breath condenses when they're lying in bed, and they do whatever they need to do to keep warm.

 He's already in the chalet when she gets back.
 'I need a shower,' she says.
 'Need a rub down?' he asks, playfully.
 'Not now Romeo, later.'
 While she takes a shower, he grabs a beer from the

fridge and watches the news on TV. He always catches the news but never comments. She has no idea what he thinks about what's going on in the world. When the headlines are finished he switches it off and gets another beer. Maybe he doesn't have any thoughts, she wonders as she dries her hair with a towel, no reason why he should.

'Get me a beer too,' she says.

'Sure.'

He passes her a beer as she puts on her slip, his favourite red one. He gives her a lascivious look. She takes a long swig, belches and goes back into the bathroom.

'Mm, sexy,' he mocks.

She looks in the mirror and brushes her hair. Her body is not what it was but she reckons it's not bad, considering, and she knows he's still keen. Sometime she thinks he might be tempted elsewhere. He's fitter than she is, slimmer, well-toned, and she can tell other women think so too. But he's never shown signs to suggest he's interested in anyone else. He still makes her feel special.

'The walk will be finished in a week or so,' he says from the other room.

'That's good.'

'I think they should take it right up to the lighthouse though. Be a big job but worth it, I reckon.'

'Does it need to go that far?' she says coming out of the bathroom.

'Maybe, maybe not. The rocks flatten out towards the lighthouse. Be OK going walking out there in the evening, but not so great coming back in the dark. Might be worth taking it all the way up there. Safer.'

'Why don't you suggest it?'

'Maybe I will. Don't want them to think I'm creating work for the sake of it but I think it would be worth it.'

She turns her back to him so he can zip up her dress.

'That's better. It's so hot.' He kisses her neck.

'Better take a shower myself, before we go.'

'Make it a cold one.'

As he undresses and digs around for a towel under a pile of clothes, she looks out through the window across the bay. Some evening surfers stride across the beach, silhouettes against a background of sun-lit spray. She needs to tell him.

'I thought I saw him today,' she says, louder than she intended, 'just for a moment.'

'Who?'

'You know who.'

'Where?'

'In the laundry. It wasn't him, it was only Marty. I couldn't see his face properly at first.'

The man puts his hand on the woman's shoulder. She turns away from the window and rests her head on his chest. She is trying not to cry.

'I'm sorry.'

'That's OK. You're not the only one.'

He wraps her in his arms. He doesn't say it but he often sees him too, on the beach with some other adults maybe, playing in the sand, learning to surf, running in and out of the shadows of the trees. Usually from a distance, out of the corner of his eye, and only ever for a moment.

'Jim says he can ask around, see if anyone needs a carpenter up in town,' he says. 'Bound to be some work for me, what with all this building going on. If we want.'

'I thought you didn't want to do that sort of work anymore? Wanted something different, you said.'

'Sure, but maybe I need to start thinking about it. Maybe we both do. You're a good worker, plenty of experience, I'm sure you can find something as well, plenty of places opening up for visitors. If you're ready.'

'Of course, but maybe not now, not yet. Maybe in the spring. Spring would be a good time to start. New season and all that.'

'Sure, spring would be good. There's no hurry.'

He strokes her hair and she holds his bare shoulders. She likes the touch of his strong, skilful, soothing hands on her head. She wants to hold on to him harder but her right hand is still weak, has been ever since that last moment when her grip failed.

In the evening they sit out with a bunch of other volunteers by the barbeque pit at the top of the beach, drinking beer and cooking burgers. Strictly this isn't their territory but when there are no visitors around, they are allowed to be there. Tonight there's a seafood special in the restaurant so there are no visitors here, just some of the volunteers who don't work in the restaurant. Cindy's there, and Scally and Betty, his silent sullen teenage daughter, Cal who always sits next to Betty if he can which only seems to make her more sullen, and a few others. Jim's there with Marty who is fast asleep in Cindy's lap under a blanket she brought just in case.

'I see they've put up some signs on the highway,' someone says, 'warning signs.'

'What for?'

'To warn folk, I guess.'

Cal titters but no one else does. Betty scowls.

'Seriously, why else would they be there?'

'That ain't gonna be good for business.'

'Maybe it's some insurance shit. Come here at your own risk buddy, or something like that. Don't say we didn't warn you.'

'And watch out for acts of God while you're here.'

'The vengeful biblical kind.'

'Even saw a couple of visitors taking a selfie next to one of those signs. Can you imagine? Grinning away like fucking idiots.'

'I can't believe that.'

'That's sick.'

There is a brief silence. The man raises his can of beer.

'Let's not forget why we're here guys. Here's to you Jim, and Marty.'

'Jim and Marty!' They chorus.

'Thanks,' Jim says with that deep drawl that's become so familiar and reassuring, 'good to move on but I'll miss you folks.'

'We'll miss you too Jim,' the woman says, slightly drunkenly, 'you've been a rock.'

'It's only a few miles up the road for fuck's sake,' says Scally.

'But it's like a whole world away,' Cindy says, 'it feels like a different world up there now. I hardly recognise it.'

'A whole new world.'

'Hallelujah to that.'

'Isn't there a song? A whole new world. Some Disney shit?'

'Don't even go there.'

'You're all welcome to come and see us, anytime,' drawls Jim, 'maybe they'll let you use the bus and we can all go down on the pier or something. Do some crabbing. Marty'll like that.'

'Sounds good.'

'You're all welcome anytime.'

'I've got a kettle if you need one Jim,' the woman says. Jim nods thoughtfully and the woman takes a last swig of beer from her can.

When the visitors begin to leave the restaurant and head towards the beach for their evening strolls, the volunteers make themselves scarce. There are other places they could assemble but the consensus is that it's time to disperse and head back to their chalets. Some have early starts.

As they walk back to their chalet arm in arm, the man and woman are silent. It is still unusually warm. The early morning breeze didn't herald a change, and now hardly a breath of air is moving. When she was young, down south, people said a breathless night was a sign of more to come, but she doesn't want to think about that. It's been breathless now for a while.

'I'm just going to check,' she tells the man as they approach the chalet. She does this most nights, he's used to it.

As he enters the chalet, leaving the door ajar, she walks a few paces on through the trees to the edge of the beach and looks out across the ocean. It's nearly dark but she can see the long black line lying across the horizon. It's still there, she thinks, the black line. It sits between sea and sky, all across the horizon, quietly waiting. You can't take your eyes off it, she thinks. If you do, it will come in and take everything, take your child, your home, everything. The First Nations people have a name for it but I can't remember it right now. But I know it will churn you all up, churn everything up, toss you in the air, split victims from survivors, the dead from the living, wilfully, haphazardly, violently. So strong it can break a mother's grip on her child's arm. That's what it does, and there's nothing you can do.

But for now, it sits there on the horizon biding its time. It's still there and so are we, she thinks, watching each other, day after day. It won't catch us out again.

The chalet is where we live, our home, and this is how it is, she thinks walking back through the trees, how it is until things change. It's the right place. She'll know when it's time to go, but it's not yet. There's still work to do, things to clean, repair and build, things to make and make better, make well. Maybe in the spring, maybe not. As she turns away from the beach, she feels a flicker of breeze. It will be cooler tomorrow, she is sure of it.

The man is lying naked on the bed when she enters the chalet. He is wide awake, looking at her. He smiles. As she begins to undress in front of him she can see that it's already starting, and it will be good again.